Carol Anne Dobson

FREEDOM

Appledrane

APPLEDRANE

Published by Appledrane 2013
Copyright© Carol Anne Dobson

ISBN 978-0-9558324-3-7

The characters in this book are entirely the product of the author's imagination and have no relation to any person in real life.

Printed by CPI Antony Rowe, Eastbourne.

Illustration and Graphic Design by Lynda Corbett

APPLEDRANE

33 Carlton Road, TORQUAY, Devon, TQ1 1NA, England

TO XAVIER AND ALICIA

Chapter 1

The funnel of a tornado was grazing the rim of the Sandia Mountains. It whirled backwards and forwards, connecting the land to a mushroom-shaped cloud of startling whiteness, emphasising the deep black of the sky above. The day was rapidly losing all light as the storm raged westwards, enveloping the shimmering buildings and neat grid of roads which comprised the robot city of Albuquerque. Every few seconds the dark was punctuated by brilliant zig-zags of lightning, momentarily illuminating the landscape.

Logan stood at the window, watching the progress of the tornado twisting its way down from the bare rocks onto the vegetation-covered lower slopes, before swirling across the city towards his home. An ancient keyboard and computer screen flew past and smashed into a wall, followed by snaking lengths of cable and the remains of a fence. The pinyon pine opposite was abruptly stripped of its pine needles and cones, and the whole tree, in its nakedness, was transported up into the whirling vortex of air and disappeared over the roof of the neighbouring building.

"Look at that!" he exclaimed, in awe and fear. "Do you think we will be safe?"

"The wind speed is 150 miles an hour and our building can easily withstand that," said RS 752, the silver bands glinting on the wrists and shoulders of his body, even in the gloom. "The darkness of the day is an acceptable colour in such circumstances." He did not turn away from the window, but his metallic face continued to stare at the storm, as though entranced.

Logan glanced curiously at him, remembering how he had gently cared for the roadrunner bird whose wing had been broken and how he had stroked the woolly mammoth at the zoo. 'It's almost as though he is feeling something,' he thought, ' even although you would not guess from what he is saying and how he looks.'

A blizzard of hail followed in the wake of the tornado, ricocheting everywhere, cratering the dusty ground and rattling the window. Layers of hailstones transformed the usually sun-baked city into a place more resembling a northern outpost town in the depths of winter.

"I have never seen this before, but I know it has sometimes happened in the past. It is not a sign that the climate is changing or that there is a problem. There will be some damage, but it will not be of great importance," continued RS752.

"Yes, Dad," Logan muttered, running his fingers through his short, chestnut- brown hair so that it stood on end.

"I have told you many times not to call me that. I am not your father," said RS 752. "I am a scientist and you are part of an experiment to examine the behaviour of humans as they grow up."

"Consuelo's pod family have said that they are her parents and therefore they should be called Mum and Dad," retorted Logan, looking down at the head of RS752, who was much shorter than he was.

"I am a robot, not a human," replied RS752. "You were created at the Human Baby Factory and therefore it is wrong for you to call me Dad. I am Research Scientist 752, RS752 in its abbreviated form."

Logan shrugged his shoulders and asked the question which had been on his mind for some time. "When is the human experiment going to finish?"

"Your participation in it was meant to end a year ago, when you reached fifteen, but I asked for an extension," replied RS752.

"How long have you been given?" enquired Logan, his blue eyes looking anxiously at RS752.

"An extra year," replied RS752.

"So that must be nearly up now," Logan exclaimed.

"Yes," agreed RS752, in his customary monotone.

"Are you going to ask for another extension?" Logan demanded.

"I asked, but have been rejected," said RS752. "We have been assigned a new human who is two years old, whose name is Honey."

"What is going to happen to me? Where will I go?" asked Logan. "Can I stay with you, but not be part of the experiment?"

"That is classified information," replied RS752. "I cannot tell you."

At that point, RS751 entered the activity pod, carrying a plate of waffles and maple syrup. Logan sat down at the table and absentmindedly stared at his breakfast. He idly traced a pattern in the golden liquid with his knife, his thoughts elsewhere. Then he pushed the plate away.

"Aren't you going to eat?" enquired RS751. "This is your favourite molecular cookery dish and I have added an extra chemical today."

"No, Mum, I don't feel hungry. I want to know what's going to happen to me," said Logan. "Have you any idea?"

"It is classified," said RS751.

"Do not worry. We will care for you." RS752 touched him on the shoulder and Logan thought, for one moment, that he heard him say very softly, 'son,' before realising that it must be his mind playing tricks on him.

Outside the wind was howling across the icy cityscape. Two surviving pinyon pines at the road junction snapped, both crashing heavily onto the ground, their branches flapping up and down like stranded fish. Logan looked sadly at their devastated stumps, before turning his back on the storm and going into his bed pod.

On the walls RS752 and RS751 had stuck pictures they had managed to discover from somewhere. Information on them had evidently been missing, so Logan had no idea who they were, but, as usual, he forgot the bleakness of the day as he looked at their familiar faces and shapes. They were not of metal, they were clearly of the same flesh and blood as himself, although

4

dressed in very odd clothes. One lady was smiling enigmatically at him, as though she was seeing into his mind. Another lady had a halo round her head and held a naked, human baby on her lap. Logan smiled wryly, remembering his fear for many years that he too would grow a halo round his head, as this was evidently something that happened to humans. A third picture showed a man resembling a spider who was climbing down a building, whilst the fourth portrayed an odd creature, whose name, Womble, was written on the frame.

On his cabinet he had placed two pictures of his fellow humans. One was of the whole group, their arms intertwined, on a geological trip they had made to the Grand Canyon, and the other was of Consuelo, her dark curls falling over her shoulders. She was smiling, but was looking into the sun, so it was difficult to see the colour of her eyes, which, however, Logan knew were a deep brown, almost black.

"What is going to happen?" Logan murmured to her picture as he sat anxiously on his bed. "There's just us. Why are there no other humans? There obviously have been, in the past, as I have pictures of some, but why is everything classified?" His thoughts turned to the struggling insect he had seen caught in a Black Widow spider's web at the Grand Canyon. "I'm also trapped in a web of a project I don't understand and over which I have no control," he muttered grimly.

Chapter 2

Next day the storm had vanished and the intense black of the night changed to an early morning rose-brown hue. The summits of the Sandia Mountains were again shifting shades of pink and blue, the lower slopes a vivid green, whilst in the city the gleaming glass and steel buildings radiated back the rays of the sun.

Logan sat excitedly in the hoverbee as RS752 drove him to school. Destruction had been widespread. Roofs had been torn from buildings, hoverbees had been flung higgledy-piggledy, cottonwood trees had been uprooted from the banks of the Rio Grande and flung onto unlikely locations such as the top of tall buildings, or across bridges. Debris blocked many roads, making hoverbees fly higher than usual. RS752 said nothing, calmly manoeuvring the vehicle over each obstacle and finally depositing Logan some distance away from the school, as the traffic was becoming so dense it was almost impossible to negotiate.

Logan ambled slowly along the sidewalk. Blue worker robots were already busy demolishing badly damaged buildings, restoring others and clearing the streets of rubbish. He noticed an ancient computer screen and keyboard, similar to the one he had seen smash against the wall the day before. He picked up a piece of paper and saw it was an old picture, not dissimilar to the ones stuck on his bed pod walls. It featured four humans, three of whom were holding wooden frames with strings and the fourth was beating a large pot. They were wearing suits with round necks and their hair looked as though a basin had been squashed down onto their heads and roughly cut around.

"Beatles," he read out from the caption below the image. "No," he said to himself. "Beetles are a sort of insect, not a human." He was shaking with excitement at finding a picture of other humans and quickly smoothed the paper and put it in his pocket. More scraps of paper fluttered past and he grabbed at two. 'Wall Street Crash' one had the title, whilst the other showed an unfamiliar robot standing in a desert and had the title 'One small step for man, one giant leap for mankind.' Logan looked more carefully at the image, his heart pounding rapidly. He was not sure it actually was a robot. It had a robot suit, but somehow appeared human. The words also seemed incomprehensible. He placed it in his pocket and ran rapidly along the sidewalk, no longer taking the route to school, but following the trail of old papers.

Out of breath, he stopped short at a high, steel fence. He walked quickly round its perimeter and came to a gate which had been opened to admit a cleaning machine and a file of worker robots. He glanced towards the interior and saw a low building whose roof had been completely demolished and in whose small courtyard tangled remnants of antiquated machines were submerged in piles of papers, which were being taken up by the strong wind into the sky and carried across Albuquerque.

He looked at the sign attached to the gate and blinked in surprise to see the words, 'Human History Archives.'

He did not linger, but strode quickly round the corner, trying to distance himself from the place, his instinct telling him that this was forbidden territory. His questions about humans had never been answered. He had no idea where they had come from or where they had lived, and knew he had to be cautious if he wanted to discover more.

He glanced across the road and saw that worker robots were standing still, looking at him and speaking on their communication devices. He sprinted towards the intersection and blindly raced left. He ducked down a side alley and found himself in a dark street, very different to the wide avenues and tall buildings in the rest of the city. The sidewalk was only of bare earth, and giant bodies of prickly pear cactus were growing in spiky clumps on the path, creating a barrier. Hanging, leafy tendrils of trumpet vine and honeysuckle were trailing from the wall, their flowers sweetly fragrancing the air. A hummingbird was hovering, its wings rapidly beating, making a trilling sound, the iridescent colours round its throat glittering rainbow-like as the sun caught them, disappearing as the bird moved, only to brightly flash again as it darted to a different honeysuckle flower.

On one side was a pale red adobe wall which was badly cracked. A siren suddenly blared out and robot voices could be heard nearby. He quickly edged through the gap and found himself in a shell of a small house. Part of the roof was missing, replaced by a pinyon pine, providing a shelter made by nature, its domed shape shading the ground from the sun. Giant, sword-leaved yucca plants, white blossoms flowering from their tips, guarded a doorway, whilst in a corner a red snake with white and black bands, was slithering under a stone. A tiny lizard scurried over his foot, and on a crumbling window sill hunched a delicate- green, praying mantis. Logan stood gazing in amazement at the ruined house alive with creatures and plants, which in no way resembled the sterile environment of the rest of the city, where it was rare to see even a fly or a spider.

He ran his hand over the adobe wall, feeling its powdery texture. He noticed markings on it and as he peered closely, could make out the words, 'Felipe Mendoza 1898.'

"A human was here!" he muttered. "A human whose name was 1898." The other words baffled him and he stood in the middle of the ancient building looking carefully to see if there were any more markings.

He jumped as a siren blended with the buzzing of distant hoverbees. "I must get to school," he muttered, "before they find that I'm missing." He gave a last look around him, picked up the lizard and put it in his pocket, then wriggled back through the gap in the wall and into the alley, where he gingerly squeezed past the prickly pear cactus.

He peered out into the street and saw two robots walking jerkily towards the Human History Archives building. He watched their progress for a few minutes and then strode casually out onto the sidewalk. He gave a quick glance back into the alley, then sprinted as fast as his long legs would take him in the direction of his school.

Chapter 3

The midday sun was fierce as he finally reached the school. He wiped his sweating face with his sleeve and walked slowly up the steps and into the cool of the teaching area where nine faces turned questioningly towards him as he sat down next to Consuelo. The teacher robot took no notice of his arrival and continued to give the lesson as though nothing had happened, and was explaining the flaws of the equation $E=mc^2$ when booted feet could be heard heavily approaching along the corridor. The door slid open and two grey-bodied soldier robots with black visor helmets, stepped across the threshold. TR518 stopped speaking in mid-sentence and there was an apprehensive silence in the room.

The two soldiers marched up to Logan. "You were seen in a classified area. Please explain," one demanded.

Logan struggled to keep from laughing at the politeness of the word, 'please' when coming from such a menacing figure. The usual monotony of each day had already been very disrupted and he could feel himself almost twitching with excitement at finding the Human History Archives building and the remains of an ancient house. He attempted to remain calm and stared confidently at the nearest soldier, finding himself at a disadvantage as he could not see the robot's eyes, which were hidden by the black visor.

"My robot father, RS752, was unable to drive me all the way to school as there was too much traffic because of the storm damage. He dropped me many blocks away and I became lost." He stood up as he spoke, so that he was on a level with the robot, which was the same height as he was, rather than the shorter stature of the other robots. "I have no idea what classified area you mean. There was no sign of any restriction."

The soldier moved closer to Logan, touching the laser weapon at his waist, and Consuelo's sharp intake of breath was audible in the room.

"Ask RS752. He can verify what I am saying," he said confidently again, knowing from his silver bands that RS752 held a senior position in the hierarchy. The image of the adobe house came into his mind and the realisation that he had stood where other humans had once been, that he finally had a link, however tenuous, with an unknown past, gave him the courage to continue to look directly at the soldier. The black visors of the robots made them seem even more emotionless than the other robots, but there was an intimidating manner about them. They stood very close to Logan, almost touching him, holding their weapons. For the first time in his life Logan realised that he was seen as a threat.

'It must be the Human History Archives building,' he thought, his spirits soaring. 'It is obviously very important to them. There is information there that it is forbidden for us to know. Perhaps, by chance I've stumbled onto something important.'

The soldiers spoke on their communicating devices and Logan recognised the voice replying as that of RS752. All robot voices generally sounded the same, but RS752's seemed slightly deeper. His intonation was different and he could be heard barking out an order authoritatively to the soldier, to leave the school and stop his interrogation.

"You are to stay in your designated area, unless you are taken elsewhere by a robot," the soldier warned Logan, staring hard at him, before wheeling around and marching out of the classroom, accompanied by the other soldier and the teacher.

Everyone waited until the noise of the boots faded into the distance, then the five girls clustered round Logan, hugging him as he sighed with relief.

"Where have you been?" Consuelo asked. "I was really worried."

"I just got lost," said Logan dismissively. "I couldn't find the way here."

"Why did they care where you had been?" asked Li curiously.

"I don't know," replied Logan, shrugging his shoulders. He smiled at Consuelo, but instead of smiling back at him, she regarded him suspiciously. He reddened under her gaze and looked down at the floor.

"What are you not telling me?" she demanded, her dark brown eyes examining him closely.

"Nothing," he repeated, but he could see she did not believe him.

"Dad told me that my part in the human experiment is meant to end soon," he said. "I am to be replaced by a little girl, called Honey."

"No, that can't be true! My parents haven't said anything to me like that!" exclaimed Consuelo. "I am sure you are wrong."

"The thing is," said Logan. "They are not our parents. We just call them that. We don't know where we come from. We're not intelligent like they are and we're not made of metal and plastic."

"We're not like them at all," cried Poppy, tossing back her long, blonde hair. "They're cold and without any feelings. I don't want to live with robots any more. You know you all think the same, although no one will say it."

The group stood silently, in shock at her words.

"So they're making new humans," continued Consuelo pensively, after a few minutes. "How are they doing that? I wonder if there are other human groups, if we're not alone, after all?"

"This is my home," wailed Rosa, tears rolling down the ebony skin of her face. "I can't leave my parents," and she agitatedly started unravelling one of the many plaits braiding her black hair.

The four boys had hung back, but now they converged on Logan. Moon, who was very thin and nearly as tall as Logan, had a worried expression on his face and took off his glasses and rubbed his eyes, whilst the eight- year old Happy, originally named Trojan, until renamed by the group because of his mischievousness and sense of fun, grinned cheerfully. Scorp, whose full name was Scorpion, sullenly glared at Logan, the sallowness of his long, narrow face not enlivened by the extreme paleness of his grey eyes. His thin body seemed fragile in contrast to Logan's broad-shouldered, sturdy frame, but his physical weakness did not appear to lessen his aggressiveness.

He jabbed his fist into Logan's chest. "What are you up to? Are you playing one of your practical jokes again? You could have got us all lasered."

"It was me they wanted, not you. You weren't in any danger and anyway it was all a mistake," shrugged Logan.

"Consuelo doesn't believe you, and nor do I." Scorp's face became even paler in anger. His eyes narrowed, his thin lips pursed together, and he advanced towards Logan, pushing him with both hands.

"Leave me alone!" shouted Logan, grabbing Scorp and shoving him violently against the wall. Scorp retaliated by punching Logan in the face, making blood spurt from his nose, whereupon Moon and the heavily-built Sky wrestled Scorp to the floor, one sitting on his head, the other on his legs, while Violeta, who was five and the youngest child, shrieked in panic.

Consuelo produced a tissue and dabbed at the blood streaming down Logan's face. "Are you alright?" she asked.

"I think I've been better," commented Logan drily, smiling at Consuelo and this time receiving a smile in return. Moon and Sky clambered off Scorp and he slowly stood up, all the time staring jealously at Consuelo trying to staunch Logan's blood.

The midday meal was a sombre affair. Scorp was isolated and ignored at the end of the table. Logan was silent and the rest of the group discussed whether they should all ask their robot parents what was going to happen to them, or whether it should be only one of them. In the end, it was decided that Consuelo and Moon would ask as they were the two oldest after Logan. Therefore, if Logan was going to have to leave the group soon because he was sixteen, it was likely that the same would also be true of them. Once the decision was made, the atmosphere lightened. Violeta snuggled up to Consuelo, who affectionately smoothed her blonde curls and held her tight.

The molecular cookery chef had excelled himself and they all voraciously ate duck in orange sauce, followed by a red jelly in the shape of a rabbit, with ice cream and pears. Consuelo reached out and touched each of the younger girls. "Don't worry," she said. "We won't be separated. We're a family."

The afternoon was very quiet. The robot teacher returned and proceeded to give a talk on the advanced civilisation of the robots. "There is nowhere on P3," he said, "where there is any disturbance or trouble. Our intelligence means that our planet is always ordered and civilised.

"Except here," muttered Moon.

Logan yawned repeatedly throughout the lesson, the words of the teacher drifting in and out of his thoughts. Moon flicked bits of paper at Sky, and Violeta fell asleep on Consuelo, her head on her shoulder.

"And that is why we exist in a perfect state, without fear or wars," finished the teacher.

"What about animals?" asked Sky. "They eat each other sometimes and they fight. You haven't made everything perfect for them."

"As you said, they are animals," replied the teacher. "I am talking about superior beings who rule our world. We are safeguarding our planet for generations of robots to come. We are not foolishly exploiting its natural resources and we live in complete harmony with each other."

Logan, his face whiter than usual, sat quietly in the hoverbee as RS752 drove him home after school. RS752 looked sideways at him, then opened a small compartment and took out a medicine sponge.

"Place that on your nose. It will help the pain," he said.

Logan glanced at him in surprise. "How did you know I was hurt? I didn't think it was obvious."

RS752 almost imperceptibly shrugged his shoulders, in a replica of Logan's often performed action, but did not reply.

Logan stared at him for a moment, then said, "Thank you for speaking to the soldier."

"It was necessary," replied RS752.

At that moment, the lizard's head popped out of Logan's pocket. It swivelled round, its eyes examining its unfamiliar surroundings.

"Where did you find that?" enquired RS752.

"Oh, on my way to school this morning," declared Logan.

"It's surprising to see it here in the city," remarked RS752. "Are you intending to keep it permanently in your pocket?"

"I thought I would keep it as a pet in my bed pod," replied Logan.

"What are you going to feed it on?" asked RS752.

"I don't know," said Logan.

"Perhaps RS751 can create a fly compote or ant puree for it to eat?" suggested RS752.

Logan looked at him and if he had not known better, he would almost have thought he was making a joke.

"Yes," he muttered, as RS752 accelerated the hoverbee over the courtyard wall and down into his parking place.

Chapter 4

Next day a hoverbus took them on a field trip to the zoo, which was several miles from Albuquerque. They hoverbuzzed across the Rio Grande on the newly built bridge named the RS591, in commemoration of the scientist who had invented the robot covering, which had been called skin. Logan stared down into the chocolate brown waters which were swirling in full flood after the recent storm. Thickets of cottonwoods, salt cedars and Russian olives were shading the ground on one side of the river from the fierce summer sun, and balls of tumbleweed were blowing in from the scrubland in such numbers, that some became caught in the hoverbus's energy box, causing it to come to a halt on the bridge. It was unheard- of for any vehicle to break down and the robot teacher appeared indecisive about what to do.

Logan watched the robot with interest. It was clearly not designed to cope with anything which deviated from the programme installed in it. Although a teacher, it was a low- level robot, not one like RS752, and if it had been human it might have been described as becoming flustered. It rushed backwards and forwards, repeating the same phrase, "We are going to the zoo," whereas clearly they were not at that point going anywhere. After a long wait, the hoverbus's energy resumed working and they buzzed off the bridge and continued the journey until they reached the steel-gated entrance.

"The teacher can tell us about quantum physics, or the universe, or thermodynamics, but is unable to make a decision when an odd situation happens," Logan remarked to Consuelo.

"You think too much," she teased, prodding him with a piece of tumbleweed, then ran off laughing, holding her straw hat onto her head, her blue dress flying out behind her, as Logan rushed after her.

The grounds of the zoo followed the wide, meandering river of the Rio Grande. Every so often small copses of mesquite, shrubs and a few cottonwoods broke the uniformity of the caged enclosures, each of which possessed only one occupant. However, in the rest of the zoo, along the paths between the cages, animal life abounded. Quails, pheasants, rabbits, squirrels and roadrunners scampered, ran or flew, and the younger children in the group chased excitedly after all of them.

They trekked past the woolly mammoth enclosure where a huge, shaggy-haired creature was standing forlornly alone in his air-conditioned glass building. The neighbouring dodo appeared similarly sad and was wandering aimlessly round its small, grassy patch. The two-horned bull-like auroch was next, followed by a giant wax model of a stegosaurus, which had four spikes on its tail, a double row of plates running the length of its spine and very short forelegs. The younger children gazed in delight, but Moon looked disenchanted.

"Why isn't there a real one?" he asked.

"Because dinosaurs are extinct," replied the teacher.

"But surely all these animals are extinct?" remarked Logan. "So how are they here?"

The teacher did not reply, as was often the case when Logan asked a question, and quickly moved on to the sabre-toothed tiger enclosure. Logan, Consuelo and Violeta meandered slowly along, Consuelo giggling as she put a daisy in her hair and threaded another one in Violeta's blonde curls. They reached the second- to-last enclosure, with its captive inmate a broad-faced potoroo, a grey and white marsupial resembling a large rat with very puffy cheeks, which Violeta wanted to take home with her. Logan and Consuelo left her clutching the cage, blowing kisses to the creature, and wandered beyond it to the last enclosure which was much larger than the others. A long strip of dusty ground extended to the south where there were a series of low buildings towards the far perimeter. It was surrounded by a steel fence along which surveillance cameras were mounted at regular intervals, a very unusual feature, as apart from a few traffic cameras, the peaceful nature of robot society meant there was no need to spy on its citizens.

"That's strange," remarked Consuelo. "I've hardly ever seen those before."

There was no animal visible, the buildings appeared uninhabited, and Logan peered through a chink in the fence to try and see more clearly what was going on. His face touched the steel and he jumped back in shock.

21

"Ouch!" he exclaimed, holding his throbbing cheek. "It's electrified! It must be a very dangerous creature in there."

"It might be lots of creatures, as there are many buildings," said Consuelo.

She and Logan again tried to look through the narrow slits in the fence, but it was impossible to see anything other than a few scrubs and cactus.

"Perhaps we can return another time to see what the animal is," said Logan.

Consuelo looked at the river. "Do you remember when we were very young and we went on a picnic to some trees over there?" and she pointed to a bend some distance downstream.

"No," replied Logan. "No, I can't remember."

"We ate raspberries from the bushes and it was the first time we had real food and not molecular cookery," said Consuelo.

"Oh yes, I remember that now," said Logan.

"And I fell into a deep hole. There was a large, underground chamber and I was very frightened because it was so dark," continued Consuelo.

"Yes, I remember that as well," said Logan laughing. "You were covered in mud when they got you out. Let's see if we can find any more berries on the bushes here and perhaps you can try not to fall down any holes."

Consuelo, Violeta and Logan wandered happily together through the zoo grounds, only joining the others when the sun was starting to sink in the west and the brilliant blue of the sky was changing to a vibrant red and yellow.

Chapter 5

Logan jumped out of bed immediately after dawn. He looked towards the Sandia Mountains and saw that the light was already changing them into shades of purple and blue with a faint glimmer of pink at their crests. His packed rucksack was ready by the door and he had just put on his shirt and trousers when RS752 entered the bed pod.

"You will be given instructions from your teacher when you arrive at the camping area, but I want to speak to you now." He looked at Logan who was putting on his walking boots and heaving the rucksack onto his back.

"Would you stop and pay attention to my words. You are not leaving until I have talked to you."

Logan grimaced with impatience, but interrupted what he was doing and sat down on the bed.

"It is dangerous in the mountains. You have to be careful. Your teacher will tell you what to do if you see a bear or a cougar, so I will not repeat his words. You will be alone without a robot for five days and this will be a new experience for all of you."

Logan stared and ran his fingers through his shock of dark chestnut hair in surprise. "I did not realise we would be on our own. We have never been allowed to do that before."

"Yes, that is so. This will be different to anything you have done." RS752 waited a moment, as though he was thinking. "I want you to take these two things with you. You are to keep them secret. You are not to tell the others or any robot. Do you understand?"

Logan looked at him. "Yes, Dad," he replied solemnly, and on this occasion RS752 did not correct him.

RS752 held out a laser gun. It was the first time Logan had seen him with a weapon. He was not a soldier robot, he was a scientist, and it was unknown for an intellectual to carry a gun. Logan took it hesitantly, almost shocked that that he, a human, was being handed a weapon.

"I'm not a robot, why are you giving it to me?"

"It is just in case you need it to protect yourself."

"Are the animals that dangerous?" Logan enquired, a nervous edge to his voice.

"They are not if you behave in the correct fashion, but there might be other dangers...." RS752's monotone voice hesitated. Logan received the distinct impression that his robot father was unwilling for him to go on the camping trip and he stared at him in surprise.

"If something is attacking you and you are in grave danger, press this button to activate the gun. It is very powerful and will kill either an animal or a human, so do not use it unless it is absolutely essential to protect yourself. It is also against robot law for me to give it to you, so as I have said, please keep it secret."

He handed Logan the other object he was carrying and Logan saw that it was a communication device. "Again, this must be kept secret from the others, including your teacher. If you need help, press this part here," and he pointed to a red square, "and you will instantly be able to talk to me."

He glanced at the lizard which was sitting on the bedside cabinet sunning itself in the early morning rays. "I will care for your pet while you are away."

"Thank you, Dad," said Logan, his voice choked with emotion. He put his arm round RS752 and hugged him, in the same way he was used to hugging the others in his group. This time, however, he came into contact with the hard metal and plastic of RS752's body, and not the warmth of human flesh, and it seemed a very strange sensation.

"Put them in the pocket of your trousers and keep them safe," ordered RS752, before escorting Logan down through the building to the sidewalk to await the rest of the group.

Chapter 6

The hoverbus buzzed over the road leading to the foothills. Logan gazed out at the short prairie grass, occasionally glancing to the back seat where Scorp had managed to sit next to Consuelo, annoying both himself and Violeta. Sky had taken a whole seat to himself as his large body could not easily be squeezed into one place, and Moon was teasing the rest of the girls, with the help of Happy, who was always his accomplice. Flowers were everywhere, black-foot daisies, white prairie-clover and baby asters, splashing colour amongst the different shades of green. The hoverbus was cool, but outside the temperature was already climbing steeply and two golden eagles were soaring in the currents of warm air.

The hoverbus reached the foothills, now travelling more slowly as it had to leave the road and buzz over dry, dusty scrublands. Scarlet globe-mallow and yellow spine-thistle could be seen amongst the distinctive trees and shrubs of the arid region, and Apache plume, plains prickly- pear, yucca and rubber rabbit-brush meant the vehicle had to hover much higher than in the city.

Logan touched the gun in his pocket, slightly reassured by it, but also worried that RS752 had felt the need to give it to him. He sat quietly in his seat, the thought occurring to him that he was now keeping a second secret from Consuelo. He glanced back to her seat and it disconcerted him to see she was chattering and laughing with Scorp.

The scrub of the foothills changed to a more dense covering of vegetation, although there was still a profusion of wild flowers. Mountain mahogany, pinyon pine and alligator juniper were everywhere, shading the ground from the sun. The hoverbus halted in a clearing and the group peered out from the windows to see a collection of tents and a concrete area where there was already a fire burning in spite of the heat of the day. Sky was first out of the hoverbus, quickly followed by the others, and they all stood breathing in the pine-fragranced mountain air.

The robot teacher stood by the tents giving instructions. "There are wild animals here which can be dangerous. Do not wander off into the forest. Always stay on the trails. When you are walking along, talk and make a noise to let a bear know you are there. If a bear stands upright it is trying to see, hear and smell you better. Just walk along slowly. If a bear or a cougar attacks you, fight back with a stick or a stone."

"I want to go home," cried five-year-old Violeta. "I don't want to meet a bear or a cougar and attack them with a stick."

The teacher ignored her and continued to talk. "Keep the trash in a clean and closed container, inside a metal box, and place it a long way from the tents. You will be on your own for five days and you need to work together as a group in order to stay safe. Do not let the fire go out, but do not attempt to move it elsewhere. Your food for the whole time is over there," and he pointed to a concrete pillar in the trees. "Use it wisely. Don't eat the…." The robot's words trailed off and with that he stepped back into the hoverbus which promptly buzzed off down the hill in the direction of Albuquerque, whose white buildings could be seen from the encampment.

"Don't eat the what?" questioned Li.

"I think it was a malfunction. I've seen it once before," said Logan. "One day I saw a worker robot going round in circles sweeping the sidewalk." He looked at Consuelo and she looked uneasily back at him. The others appeared subdued. A branch cracked underneath a giant Ponderosa pine and Violeta screamed and jumped into Logan's arms.

"It's alright, it's nothing," said Logan, uncertainly looking across at the pine, and depositing her on a large stone, whereupon she continued to cling to his trouser leg.

"It's odd, isn't it," exclaimed Scorp, "that they've left us on our own like this. We're never allowed to go anywhere, or do anything, unless it's with a robot, and now they've suddenly abandoned us up here in this wilderness for five days."

"It's exciting, but weird at the same time," said Sky.

"It's an experiment," Scorp suddenly exclaimed. "But an experiment for what?"

Consuelo went to the concrete store block to discover the food rations and came back bearing mallows. "Find some sticks," she said, "and we can toast them."

Twigs were located, mallows stuck on the ends, and the group sat quietly round the fire trying to enjoy themselves, but not really succeeding. It was an extremely hot day and everyone was soon sweating profusely. The mallows were gulped down and they abandoned the fire to find coolness below the trees. A stream was trickling down the hillside into a narrow gully adjacent to the camp and they perched on flat stones, dangling their bare feet in the crystal water.

Nobody explored further than the area next to the campsite, and nightfall found the group huddled beside the fire. The long strands of grey-green lichen dangling from tree limbs waved eerily in the rose- pink glow of evening and it was almost a relief to everyone when the blackness of night abruptly descended. The stars twinkled in the heavens and the sparkling lights of Albuquerque, near the bottom of the foothills, were both a cheerful and sad reminder of home.

Chapter 7

Logan crawled out of his sleeping bag at sunrise and went to look at the fire which was still burning and appeared to be fuelled by a chemical substance in a container underneath it. Consuelo came out of her tent, yawning and stretching, still half-asleep. She sat next to Logan and they both watched the day begin. Birds were singing, animals were scuttling in the nearby undergrowth, and Consuelo glanced round her with satisfaction.

"Do you realise that everything here is alive? We are living beings and we are surrounded by other living beings. There are no robots."

"Yes," agreed Logan. "I was just thinking that. Up here in the mountains we seem to belong, whereas the robots are artificial and different."

"We couldn't live without robots," said Consuelo. "We wouldn't have clothes or food or shelter."

"Well, if there were more of us, we would manage, I'm sure," Logan declared.

"Did you ask your parents if you're going to be part of the human experiment programme now that you're sixteen?" he continued.

"Yes, I did," answered Consuelo unhappily. "They said it was classified."

"Well, at least it sounds as though we will be together," said Logan reassuringly. "It's probably best not to tell the younger ones as they might worry."

Poppy and Li emerged from their tent, soon followed by the others, and the first day of being alone, without robot supervision, began.

"I think we need to elect a leader," said Consuelo. "It's much easier if someone takes responsibility for decisions."

"That's a good idea," agreed Li. "Who would like to be in charge?"

"I would be happy to do it," said Scorp quickly.

"I would also like to be leader," declared Logan.

"We will vote," said Consuelo. "Hands up who wants Logan."

She put up her hand, as did Li, Violeta, Sky, Rosa and Moon.

"That's settled then," she said. "There's only three left to vote for Scorp."

Scorp scowled, kicked a stone at a tree and marched off into the bushes. Logan shrugged his shoulders and proceeded to give his first instructions to the group.

"I don't think the teacher robot adequately made clear the dangers yesterday. Don't touch a plant with shiny green leaves in groups of three. It's called poison ivy and can give you a terrible, itching rash. Don't go near a dead rodent in case they have fleas, as they sometimes carry an illness called bubonic plague, and, lastly, don't eat anything, even if it looks edible." He bent down and picked a small mushroom growing at his feet. "This, for instance, is an earthstar mushroom. It looks pretty, but can make you very ill if you eat it."

He stopped for a moment and looked round at everyone, then continued, "The main thing is to always stay together. It's useful to carry a stick. Let's get ourselves ready and go and explore." He spoke enthusiastically and with knowledge, and the group instantly became cheerful, the young ones running round the tents, shrieking with excitement as they had done at the zoo. Consuelo put her hand in Logan's. "Well done. You've made everyone feel better." She smiled at him and they both failed to see Scorp who was watching them from behind a tree, hatred in his eyes.

They rambled upwards, following an ancient trail between thick fir trees, slender trunks of aspens and squat-bodied oaks. Raspberry and snowberry bushes lined the path and Logan let everyone try the raspberries.

"Don't touch the snowberries," he said. "I'm not sure, but I don't think they are edible."

Flowers dotted the ground. Blue harebells and irises competed for space and orange and yellow wallflowers brightened every niche and cranny of the rocks and cliffs. The small group of humans gazed at the countryside in silence. The rich and varied beauty of the land was overwhelming and when Consuelo spoke, her voice was husky with emotion,

"It's wonderful. I can't believe we're here. It's so different to Albuquerque."

The bandit-mask face of a raccoon peered at them from an overhanging crag, a black and white skunk rushed through the undergrowth, and everywhere were deer, squirrels, chipmunks and rabbits. The younger children lost their fear. No bears or cougars were sighted, although Sky thought he saw bear prints near a muddy stream, and at the end of the day they traipsed happily back down the trail to the campsite. Scorp remained at the back of the group, speaking to no one and when they returned to the camp he went off into the undergrowth and could be heard breaking sticks and throwing stones.

Moon and Poppy started climbing a young oak tree and Consuelo called to them to come down. Poppy held onto a branch swinging backwards and forwards, steadily gaining momentum. Her hand slipped and she partly fell, before managing to grip the branch again, whilst at the same time dislodging a metal object which clattered onto the stones below.

Consuelo picked it up. "What's this?" she exclaimed, turning it over in her hand. "It's an eye!" she said in amazement, giving it to Logan.

"It is a sort of eye," he said. "Look, it can swivel round and see in every direction. I think it's a camera."

There was silence. They all suddenly realised why the robots had appeared to leave them alone. They were being watched and their faces showed their shock.

"Is it still functioning?" asked Poppy.

"I don't know," replied Logan, regarding the eye with distaste. "If it is, I expect it will enjoy the view," and with that he launched it over the hillside and into the gully.

"I wonder if there are more?" said Consuelo.

"We can have a look, but it would be impossible to find them with all these branches and leaves," he replied.

The enjoyment of the day had become tainted by the find, and the second night around the campfire was almost as subdued as the first. Scorp ate his food in his tent still refusing to speak to Logan, and after they had eaten, Happy and Poppy joined him and their loud laughter and conversation could be heard echoing strangely in the night air.

Chapter 8

Day two at the camp dawned as colourfully as day one, and Logan, Li and Consuelo sat together, watching the sunrise, seeing the orange and yellow-streaked sky gradually change into an azure blue. A luminous moon still hung like a ghost in the heavens, and as Logan looked at it, he noticed a pink and white flash erupt on its surface.

"What's that?" he exclaimed and pointed it out to Consuelo and Li.

"That's strange," said Li. "It's as though there's an explosion on the moon. That can't be so."

They watched it for a moment as it gradually faded and finally disappeared.

Scorp came out of his tent for breakfast and was once more speaking to everyone except Logan. He, Happy and Poppy disappeared into the neighbouring gully and returned to say they had found bear prints.

"That's very near our camp," cried Consuelo in horror. "Suppose it had come into our tents when we were sleeping?"

The whole group clambered over the rocks into the steep-sided ravine and clustered round large foot prints in mud by the stream. Stones and stumps had been overturned and an aspen tree had claw marks ripping open its trunk.

"Well, it looks as though it might be a bear," said Logan in dismay. "It's best not to come down here again. It's possible there's a den up there in that outcrop of rock," he said, looking up at the side of the cliff. The camp shouldn't have been placed so near to a stream, as bears like to wallow in water or catch fish. I'll try and keep awake tonight to keep guard."

He peered at the crags, but nothing moved.

"There's a cave up there," said Poppy, pointing to a dark hole by an overhanging ridge. "Could that be a den?"

"Probably not," said Consuelo briskly, and shepherded Violeta and Li back over the rocks, quickly followed by everyone else. Logan put his hand in his pocket to feel the cold steel of the laser gun, and saw Scorp glance at him thoughtfully.

They spent the morning rambling up through copses of Ponderosa pines and oaks, towards the summit of a low hill, Logan carrying Violeta on his shoulders. The day was suffocatingly hot and by midday they had drunk most of the water in their flasks.

"It's best to retrace our steps," said Consuelo. "We can't run out of something to drink."

Reluctantly, they followed the trail back down the mountainside and arrived at the camp by early afternoon. The heat was oppressive, the outline of the trees and bushes shimmering in a haze and everyone lay languidly in the shadow of an umbrella-shaped pine. Everyone except Scorp. He rummaged through his rucksack, then disappeared into the woods and was not seen again until it was time to eat, when he emerged from the trees red-faced and sweating, a streak of blood staining his shirt, his face dirty with mud.

"Where have you been?" asked Happy.

Scorp gave him a sullen stare, snatched his share of the food from Consuelo and tore at it ravenously with his teeth, like an animal, alone outside his tent.

The sun set quickly. A cool breeze finally blew down from the crests of the mountains, stirring the trees and bushes and whipping up small clouds of dust.

"I want to stay here for ever," declared Violeta, who had smeared stripes on her face with earth and stuck a black feather in her hair. "We're like a proper family."

"Yes, we're a family," said Sky, who had also decorated his face in a similar fashion. "We don't just see each other at school. We're together in the evenings and nights."

Contentment had replaced the fear of the bear. Night enveloped the camp and Consuelo hugged and kissed all the children, tucking them up in their sleeping bags, before going to sleep herself. Logan was the last to zip up his tent. He sat upright in his sleeping bag, struggling to remain awake. He took out the laser gun from his pocket, ran his hand over its smooth metal and placed it under his pillow. "Just in case," he muttered, as his eyes slowly shut.

In the middle of the night he awoke. He seemed to be rocking backwards and forwards and suddenly realised something was knocking against his tent, making a snuffling, grunting noise. He quickly flicked on his torch to see what was happening and the large head of a bear, with a black snout and glittering eyes was caught in the beam of light. He jumped out of his sleeping bag and scrabbled desperately to find the laser gun under his pillow, his hand shaking. His fingers closed round the steel and he held it firmly with both hands, aiming at the bear. The bear stopped briefly, sniffing at the dead body of a squirrel which was lying just inside the tent. He swallowed the squirrel whole and Logan could smell its rancid breath and see its strong yellow teeth in its gaping mouth. The bear lurched towards him, grunting and roaring, and Logan pressed the button on the gun, just as the huge paw of the bear shredded the side of his face with its claws.

The bear gave a roar and toppled backwards, ripping the canvas and falling half- in and half- out of the tent. His large bulk quivered, then lay still. Logan scrambled to his feet, firing repeatedly at the prostrate animal in panic and desperation to make sure that it did not unexpectedly rear up and attack again. The tent had already collapsed around him and he pushed his way out of its tattered remains, trembling in fright, blood pouring from his wounds, and stood gratefully for a few seconds looking up at the stars twinkling in the clear night sky.

The others came rushing out of their tents. Violeta, Poppy and Rosa all shrieking with terror as they saw the bear splayed out in front of them. Logan hurriedly stuffed the gun in his pocket and turned to face them.

Consuelo put her arm around him and led him to a stone to sit down. "Are you alright? Have you killed it?" she asked calmly.

"Yes," he replied. "It attacked me in the tent. There was a dead squirrel in there and it could smell it."

"A dead squirrel in your tent!" she exclaimed in horror.

They both turned and looked at Scorp, who was standing next to the body of the bear.

"Don't look at me! I had nothing to do with it!" he sneered. "How did you kill it?" he said suspiciously. "How did a human like you kill a bear?"

"I attacked it with a rock," said Logan firmly. "It came up close and I hit it on its snout."

"You're a liar! You couldn't possibly kill it with a rock. Are you using some sort of magic?"

"Don't be stupid!" cried Logan.

Scorp ignored him and prodded the bear with his foot, trying to turn it over. Its huge bulk resisted his attempts, but the movement released some air still in its body and it gave out a low, rasping grunt, as though it was alive.

The girls screamed again and ran into the trees and Logan jumped up from the stone, his hand reaching into his pocket for the gun.

The bear, however, lay prostrate, completely lifeless, and Scorp proceeded to poke it with a stick.

"Leave it alone!" cried Logan. "Go over to your tent and don't come near me!"

"Don't you threaten me!" shouted Scorp, but as Logan advanced menacingly towards him, his face, hands and clothing bloodied, he slouched off to his tent and crawled inside.

Consuelo went to find the medicine box she had seen in the concrete pillar and came back with antiseptic and bandages.

"Let me see your face," she said to Logan. "You had better sit down."

He sat again on the stone and tried to hold himself still.

"I think it will sting," she warned him. "Hold this branch tight, while I bathe it."

He sat as quietly as he could whilst she poured the antiseptic over the cuts on his face and then gently cleaned the skin with a medicinal sponge. Logan groaned, clenching his teeth together, his body trembling.

"There, I'm finished," said Consuelo. "I'll make you a hot drink with sugar in it. I think you're in a state of shock."

She looked curiously at the bear, then at Logan. "How did you kill it?" she asked.

Logan glanced at her. "I killed it," he said. "It doesn't matter how. The important thing is I killed it or I wouldn't be here speaking to you."

Consuelo regarded him with a serious expression, her eyes troubled.

"I'm sorry," he told her. "I can't say. I don't want to lie to you."

"Don't worry," she said, wrapping a blanket round him. "Perhaps you can tell me another time. I'll go and retrieve the little ones from the wood," and she smiled at him, the olive skin of her face, however, almost as pale as Logan's, and went off to find the girls.

Logan sat shivering in the blanket and looked up to see Happy staring at him. Happy said nothing, just continued to stare, almost as if he was examining a specimen in a laboratory. He looked at the bear and bent down to smell it.

"It's as though it's been lasered," he said coldly. "Have you a weapon?" There was mistrust and suspicion in his words. The mischievous, cheerful little boy seemed to have vanished and been replaced by the body of a child, who had the air of an adult. Logan glanced at him in surprise and Happy's face burst into a smile. "I'm so glad nothing happened to you," he said, touching Logan on the shoulder.

No one returned to their tents. They huddled together in the sharp coldness of the night, their sleeping bags wrapped round their shoulders, and sitting as close to the fire as possible. A large moon glowed luminously in the clear sky, the planet Venus shining with such brilliance it eclipsed even its neighbouring star constellations. On the fringe of the camping area lay the shadowy bulk of the bear, illuminated now and then by the flickering flame of the fire. A coyote howled nearby, then a second; an unknown animal scuttled squeaking through the undergrowth, there was a sudden movement by a bush and it abruptly stopped in mid-squeak.

The night was not quiet, it throbbed and rustled, and the humans glanced fearfully into the soft darkness below the trees and bushes, where indistinct shapes flickered and moved. They held sticks and stones in their hands, and the smallest children were placed nearest the fire, so that they could not be easily snatched by a marauding animal, attracted by the scent of the dead bear.

Logan guiltily felt the gun in his pocket, knowing that it would give comfort to the others to know about it, but not admitting he had it out of loyalty to his robot father. His head hurt, he felt nauseous, and when he attempted to stand, the stars and moon coalesced into one twinkling mass.

41

Finally, a lemon-yellow band of colour on the eastern horizon announced the coming of the sun. The familiar sight of the Ponderosa pines, oaks, aspen and mesquite emerged from the blur of the night shadows and blue-purple cirrus clouds trailed across the brilliance of a pink and yellow sky.

Consuelo heated beans and tortillas in a pan over the fire. She also brewed coffee, its aroma drifting over the camp site, luring Scorp out of his tent. Logan held the mug of coffee in his hand, the warmth returning to his body, and glanced at Scorp nonchalantly eating breakfast next to Poppy and Happy, as though innocent of any wrong doing. Violeta moved fearfully next to Consuelo and the muted conversation that had been taking place stopped.

Logan addressed Scorp. "You put the dead squirrel in my tent, didn't you? You wanted me to be attacked."

"No, I didn't! You're trying to smear me! It probably just wandered into your tent and the smell killed it!"

"What you did was dangerous. The bear might have gone on to attack other people after me," said Logan furiously. He and Scorp glared at each other, the usual friction between them escalating to a new level.

He strode towards Scorp, who stepped backwards.

"You're a coward!" shouted Logan. "You're yellow through and through. All you care about is yourself. It doesn't bother you that you put everyone here in danger!"

"It's not true! You think too much of yourself!" cried Scorp. "We've always got to do what you want and what you say. I think it's time to change the leader now that you've been hurt. You're not strong enough." With that he picked up a large branch and held it threateningly at Logan.

Logan charged him and they fell onto the ground, rolling over and over in the dust. He hammered Scorp repeatedly with his fists and Scorp staggered to his feet and ran away in to the forest.

"Stop! Let him go!" cried Consuelo, but Logan paid no notice and pursued Scorp, quickly gaining on him.

Scorp seemed to know where he was going. He ran surefootedly amongst the trees, leading Logan into a part of the forest he had not seen. They came to a grassy slope leading to bare rock and Scorp stopped and turned around, taunting Logan to come close to him. There was a cunning look in his eyes and for a moment Logan hesitated. Then his anger overcame him and he charged Scorp. Scorp stepped aside and violently pushed Logan over the precipice. Logan lost his footing and found himself tumbling down the cliff side. He grabbed desperately at bushes to try and break his fall, but the plants were spindly and brittle and snapped in his hands. Finally, the branch of a small tree held his weight and he hung in the air, flailing his legs and trying to find a foot- hold on the smooth rock. Far below, white-foaming rapids were cascading through a gorge and he tried to avoid looking down.

He glanced up and saw Scorp's pale face peering down at him, as the branch he was holding began to crack and splinter, clearly only seconds away from breaking.

He abandoned the branch, inching his way up the side of the cliff, sweat streaming down his face and stinging the cuts from the bear. He struggled upwards, cursing his foolishness in straying into unfamiliar terrain and letting himself be fooled by Scorp, and continued to climb steadily, finally reaching a rocky overhang below the grass.

"Take my hand," called out Scorp, his white face with its close-set eyes abruptly appearing again over the cliff edge.

"No!" Logan angrily called out, unable to trust the intentions of his unlikely rescuer. "Get back! If you touch me I'll pull you over as well," he threatened.

The next minute, Sky's black face and curly hair replaced that of Scorp. He was holding onto a stunted aspen tree and gradually extended his hand down to Logan and grabbed his shirt. He hauled him up over the overhang, his bulky body and the tree taking Logan's weight as he scrambled upwards, before being pulled finally over the edge by Sky. He lay panting on the grass, looking up at the faces of the whole group, who had frantically followed the pair as they had run through the wood. The world spun dizzily round him and he fainted.

Chapter 9

He regained consciousness at the camp. He was lying on a sleeping bag in a tent and Violeta was sitting next to him. Her brown eyes looked worriedly at him for a moment, then she ran outside, calling to Consuelo.

"How did I get here?" asked Logan, as she appeared in the entrance.

"We all carried you," she said. "You were very heavy," and she smiled happily.

"Where is Scorp?" Logan asked.

"He's here," she said. "He came back with us."

"He tried to kill me again," said Logan. "He's very dangerous."

"You can't be sure he had anything to do with the squirrel," said Consuelo. "Perhaps it just happened to come into your tent."

"It was dead!" Logan protested, "And he pushed me off the edge of a cliff!"

"Well, again, you can't be sure. You were both fighting and it all happened in the heat of the moment. It was wrong of you to hit him in the first place," remarked Consuelo bluntly.

Logan looked angrily at her. "Don't be taken in," he exclaimed. "You always think the best of everyone, but in the case of Scorp, you are wrong, and he might try and hurt you."

"Stop being cross," Consuelo replied. "I think you've had enough injuries and excitement for one day. Just stay here quietly in the tent and I'll look after everyone."

Sky put his face through the entrance to the tent and grinned at Logan.

"Are you alright?" he asked.

"Yes, thanks to you," Logan said, holding out his hand and clasping Sky's large fist.

"I think we've a problem with the bear," Sky replied. "It's going to smell in the heat and we've still two days to go. We're also at risk of animals coming to eat the carcass and vultures are already gathering. Do you think the robots have seen what's happened, with other cameras than the one we found, and will come and rescue us? Do you think we should leave and start to walk back down the mountain?"

"I don't know," said Logan. "They haven't come yet, so I would think that they don't know about it. On the other hand, we have no idea why we're here on this camping trip and what they want from us. As for returning by ourselves, it's a long way down for the younger ones"

He gingerly climbed out of his sleeping bag, ignoring Consuelo's orders, and went out of the tent. He glanced grimly at the bear, and then at the sky, where three turkey vultures were soaring in ever-decreasing circles high above the carcass. One flew down and landed on the ground next to the bear, its pink head and curved beak poised to bite into the flesh. Logan ran towards it, waving his arms and the huge bird took off again into the sky, its black, white and grey wings spreading out into their familiar V-shape.

Scorp, Happy and Poppy were standing together near the woods and all three looked coldly towards him. Logan glared briefly at Scorp and sat down shakily next to Rosa, who smiled welcomingly.

"We need to get rid of the bear's body somehow," Logan said. "It's too far to push it over the cliff and in any case it will attract animals and vultures, and the ravine is not all that far from our camp."

He stood up and wandered over to the bear, watched in an unrepentant and unfriendly manner by Scorp.

"We could burn it with the fire," suggested Violeta.

Logan looked at the five-year-old in surprise. "What a good idea!" he exclaimed. He glanced at the fire and stood lost in thought for a few minutes. "The fire has obviously got to be built here," and he pointed to a bare, dusty patch, halfway between the tents and the trees. "Can you all go and find sticks and branches."

Scorp, Happy and Poppy stood apart, frowning at him, but everyone else busied themselves, rushing backwards and forwards, collecting as much brushwood as they could find. They heaped it next to Logan and he fashioned into a pyramid. His face was beginning to swell from the claw marks, and several times he had to sit down to stop from fainting.

He picked up the strips of ripped material from his tent and tied it round the two hind legs, wrinkling his nose as he did so from the odour emanating from the carcass. "I don't know if it always smells like this," he exclaimed, "or whether it's the heat making it decompose."

He, Sky, Moon and Consuelo pulled the bear across the ground, dropping it roughly on its funeral pyre. He picked up a twig and lit it from the fire, shielding it carefully with his hand from the wind, to prevent it being extinguished. He placed the burning twig inside the heaped brushwood and blew vigorously to catch it alight. Sparks crackled from the wood, the small group of humans crowding round in fascination as the bonfire blazed with a loud, whooshing noise. Smoke poured from the base, engulfing the spread-eagled bear and making everyone cough and splutter.

Logan looked with satisfaction at his handiwork and at the back of the bear, which had no sign of laser scorch marks, unlike the tell-tale marks he knew were on its front.

The wind was shifting direction and blowing strongly from the plain towards the mountains. A sagebrush bush near to the fire suddenly burst into flame, then so did another one, and a spark fell on the nearest tent. It did not burn, it just melted and spread out into a puddle. The leaves on the nearest tree also burst into flames and there was a strong smell of burning pine wood. The tinder- dry grass caught fire, and in a few minutes not only was the funeral pyre burning merrily, so were all the trees and bushes at one side of the wood.

Logan and the others stared aghast. "Run!" shouted Logan. "Run for your lives!" and he picked up Violeta.

The wind was fanning the fire upwards and had now caught all the tents. The heat was scorching, and burning leaves were falling onto their clothes and hair.

The air was thick with smoke, flames leaping beneath it, and in a few minutes the hillside was ablaze.

The humans raced down the hill, Consuelo tripping and falling, and as Logan stopped to help her up, they were joined by a host of animals. A black bear appeared out of the trees, his coat singed, and with a roar lumbered down the hill. Snakes emerged from stones, a herd of deer was stampeding, coyotes, rabbits and chipmunks were all scampering downwards trying to escape from the burning vegetation, whilst a host of birds rose squawking into the air. Logan briefly glanced behind him in horror at the nightmare scene, then continued to run with the others down the uneven hillside. Cacti caught against them, scratching their hands and faces, and black smoke was billowing around, making everyone gag and splutter.

"Wrap your clothes over your mouth and nose," shouted Logan, as red and orange flames shot up from the juniper tree nearest to him He stopped for a second and grabbed the communication device from his pocket. He pressed the red button and RS752 instantly answered.

"We can see the fire from Albuquerque," he said. "Vehicles are being sent now to extinguish it. Where are you? You will be rescued as quickly as possible."

"We're in the foothills, immediately below the blaze," said Logan.

"Keep the red button on. It will act as a signal and guide us to you," replied RS752.

Logan put back the communication device in his pocket, still holding Violeta, and kept on running at the speed of the slowest child, which was Poppy.

In the distance, the buildings of Albuquerque were gleaming white in the sun and the faint noise of the sirens could be heard. A V-shaped formation of army hoverwasps was fast approaching, and at its apex was the large, grey shape of the hoverhornet, the most advanced vehicle in the military fleet. They passed over the humans, droning loudly, deafening everyone. Two hoverwasps detached themselves from the squadron and landed on a patch of scrubland. Logan pulled his shirt more tightly over his mouth and nose, his lungs feeling so choked it was becoming difficult to breathe. Everyone around him was doing the same, with the exception of Happy, who appeared to be having no difficulty, even although his face was not protected by any clothing.

Soldier robots disembarked from the hoverwasps and ran towards the exhausted group of humans.

"Give me the young one," a black-visored soldier commanded Logan and took Violeta from his arms. The soldiers picked up the smallest children and carried them to the hoverwasp, whilst Logan, Consuelo, Scorp and Moon stumbled unaided across the ground and up into the welcoming safety of the hoverwasp.

Once airborne, Logan looked out of the window and was transfixed by horror to see the extent of the fire raging over the mountains. The flames were now rapidly spreading over much of the lower foothills and the smoke was so thick it was as if night had come to that part of the sky. Shame made his eyes fill with tears.

"It was my fault," he muttered to Consuelo. "It was all my fault. I didn't realise how dry the plants were. And how quickly a fire can spread."

"Don't worry," said Consuelo, holding his hand. "It was my fault as well. I didn't realise either." She lay back against the seat, her olive skin streaked with soot, her eyes red. "We will be together...." Her mouth quivered and she burst into tears.

They were taken to the Medical Centre. The girls were in one ward, Logan, Scorp, Moon and Sky in another. Logan glanced round to see where Happy was, but he seemed to have disappeared.

He was given a tetanus injection as a protection from the bear injuries, then he showered, fresh clothes were allocated to him and he joined the others in the ward.

"I told you it was stupid to light a fire," said Scorp critically.

"No, you didn't," replied Logan, unwilling even when cast down by despair, to let Scorp claim any credit."

"I wonder what they will do to you," taunted Scorp. "You're to blame."

The windows of their ward faced south, so Logan wandered to the ward of the girls, which had a view of the Sandia Mountains. Violeta jumped on him and gave him a hug and he smiled to see she was alright. Everyone was already crowded round the window and he joined them to stare at the devastated sight of the mountains, still burning furiously, in spite of the efforts of the hoverwasps and hornet to douse the flames with a chemical which was turning the fire purple and creating huge, white sparks.

Logan sank down wretchedly on a bed, his head in his hands, and the united efforts of Consuelo and the girls were unable to cheer him in any way whatsoever. He was still slumped in a state of misery when RS752 came to collect him an hour later.

"Don't say anything until we reach home," said RS752. "Come on, I think you need to rest and have some of RS751's cooking," and he helped Logan up from the bed and led him downstairs to the waiting hoverbee.

At home, RS751 had been busy with her molecular cookery, as RS752 had promised, and Logan sat at the table, treated to the delights of a meal evidently called a Thanksgiving Dinner. He voraciously tucked into the turkey, sweet potatoes and cranberry sauce, and the horror of the past few days began to fade surprisingly quickly from his mind.

"We are giving thanks that you have been safely returned to us," said RS752. "It is a very old recipe and I don't know its origin."

Logan looked around at the living pod and at his robot parents. "It's wonderful to be back," he said.

RS 752 looked at him and Logan could have sworn that there was a hint of a smile on his metallic face. He knew it could not really be so, but the thought cheered him and he hugged RS752 and RS751 at the same time.

Later, when he had eaten and rested, RS752 sat down with him and asked what had happened.

"I believe you know, partly," replied Logan. "There were hidden cameras at the site, I think, apart from the one we found."

"There were two," admitted RS752, "and you destroyed one, which was very foolish, as I had them placed there partly for your protection."

Logan looked at him in surprise. "What do you mean?" he asked.

"Humans are often violent and unpredictable," replied RS752. "It was thought that if you were alone in the wilderness, without supervision, there would not be the same peace and tranquillity that is found here in robot society."

Logan stared at him. "You are right," he said, hanging his head in shame. "I fought with Scorp as I thought he had placed a dead squirrel in my tent, and I fell off a cliff."

"How did the fire start?" enquired RS752. "I presume it had something to do with human activity."

"A bear came into my tent because it smelt the squirrel, and I killed it with the gun you gave me. Its dead body would have attracted other animals so I had to destroy it. I did not want any human, or robot, to see the burn marks and know it had been lasered, because it was illegal for you to give me the weapon, and so it seemed a good idea to burn it in a fire." He shrugged his shoulders and stared down at the floor, waiting for RS752 to speak.

There was a long silence. Logan looked up and saw RS752 staring at him.

"You were right to do what you did," said RS752. "It was a logical action on your part and was successful as far as disposing of the bear's body was concerned. The unfortunate consequences of the fire resulted from insufficient knowledge of the danger of fire in very dry countryside. For that, robots must share a part of the responsibility as you were not properly trained to deal with the situation. As far as Scorp is concerned, I do not fully understand this emotion of anger you feel towards him, but I believe he exhibits the worse traits of human nature, whereas you are responding to his threats."

Logan glanced at his robot father.

"It was also logical to want to protect me as you realised I might be harmed if it was known I had given you the gun. Although, as a robot, I am not able to feel gratitude, I believe you to have acted in a sensible and correct manner." He moved nearer to Logan and held him with both arms, in a resemblance of a hug. "You did well, my human son, and I am proud of you, even if you appear to have burnt down much of the Sandia Mountains."

At that moment, sirens sounded. Logan and RS752 moved to the window to see what was happening and found themselves looking at a large golden eagle perched on the wall at the corner of the building. In the road below a herd of deer was thundering along and robots on the sidewalk were having to take evasive action and leap into doorways. A slightly singed lone chipmunk sat on a traffic sign, and blackened leaves and plants were being blown by the wind onto the pristine streets of Albuquerque.

"I have never seen this before," said RS752. "Our society and environment is always very well-ordered. Do not go to school tomorrow. It is best that you stay here under my protection."

Logan looked at him, not sure if he meant there was a threat from the invasion of animals, or whether there was a threat of another kind." He fumbled in his pocket and gave RS752 back his gun and communication device, then settled down to watch Robot News Today on the screen in the living pod, where the fire in the

Sandia Mountains in Albuquerque was the main news item, ahead even of Sector Three being given the Nobel Peace Prize for the third year running.

"It should have been Sector Four," RS752 muttered in a monotone.

Chapter 10

The soldiers came for Consuelo before it was dawn. The knock on the door awoke her and she rubbed her eyes sleepily to see RS890, her robot mother, standing in the doorway with two grey-bodied, black-visored soldiers. "What's happening?" she asked.

"You have to go," said her robot mother. "I will pack some clothes for you to take."

"Where am I going to?" said Consuelo in panic, jumping out of bed.

"I do not know," said RS890, "but I cannot help."

"Will I see you again?" Consuelo asked, her voice shaking.

"I do not know," RS890 repeated.

Consuelo quickly dressed, placing her picture of Logan in her pocket, and gave her mother a last hug. The soldiers marched her in front of them, out of the living pod and down into the street. "Where are you taking me?" she asked again, but they remained silent. They motioned to her to climb into the hoverwasp, and she reluctantly did so, first glancing up at the window of her building where she could see RS890 gazing at her.

Consuelo gave one last despairing look before clambering into the hoverwasp. Torrential rain was pouring down and Consuelo was drenched in the few minutes she had stood in the open air. Her chest still hurt from the smoke of the fire, and a mounting sense of panic made it difficult for her to catch her breath. Her eyes filled with tears and she tried to prevent herself from crying, so that she could be fully aware of what was happening and where she was being taken.

One soldier sat next to her, the other drove the vehicle. She felt intimidated by their size and their weapons, and could not stop trembling from both fear and her wet, cold clothes. For the first time in her life she noticed that the city of Albuquerque looked dirty and untidy. Burnt leaves and plants littered the concrete, black streaks were trickling down walls and windows, and muddy pools were collecting along sidewalks and roads.

The hoverwasp turned the corner and had to rise higher in the air as a flash flood suddenly roared down the street. Rain beat onto the roof and windows of the hoverwasp, and for a moment Consuelo gazed in amazement at the power of the raging water which was carrying away signs, parts of buildings and walls.

A black bear loomed, roaring, out of the rain. The soldiers said nothing, but the hoverwasp accelerated. Even in the heavy rain the city appeared alive with wild animals. Deer were sheltering in doorways, and squirrels were running up and down walls, tracked, in one instance, by a cougar. The bizarre sights she was seeing, coupled with the strangeness of being with the soldiers, made her wonder, at one point, if she was having a nightmare and that she would wake up and find it was only a dream. She pinched herself and when it hurt, she was disappointed to discover that this was really happening.

They buzzed past the new inhabitants of Albuquerque and its rain-sodden streets, and crossed the same bridge as on the trip to the zoo. The sky was beginning to lighten and the night chill lessen. The usual chocolate colour of the Rio Grande was a drab grey. It had flooded over its banks and was snatching trees and bushes, pulling them down into its torrent, awash with debris. For a second she thought of Logan, before shutting him out of her mind and trying to concentrate on the present. They buzzed along the route she recognised as leading to the zoo and was not unduly surprised when they reached the same steel entrance they had entered before.

They stopped next to two other hoverwasps waiting in puddles of water. Scorp and Moon were standing in the rain, guarded by robot soldiers, their thin clothes as wet and bedraggled as Consuelo's. Moon was standing quietly, but Scorp started to furiously kick at the hoverwasp, and a soldier roughly pulled him away, threatening him with his laser gun. It cheered her somewhat to see them and she wondered briefly if Logan would also arrive. Her hoverwasp stopped and the soldiers motioned to her to descend.

She clambered out, tearfully greeting the others, and saw Moon was trembling as much as she was. The soldiers told them to walk and marched them along a path next to the cages. In a sudden flash of intuition she knew where they were going, seeing again, in her mind, the low buildings, the dusty ground and the electrified fence.

The rain continued to pour down. One of the soldiers made a spluttering sound and collapsed onto the ground, sparks coming from his chest, which were swiftly extinguished by the deluge. Scorp, Moon and Consuelo looked in astonishment at him. They had never before seen a robot which was not functioning. They knew the robots needed to charge themselves at regular intervals from special charging stations, but they had never seen it actually happen.

"I think the rain has penetrated his body covering," said Scorp "and blown a fuse or something."

The other robot stood still. He looked at his fallen colleague and appeared to be reflecting on the situation. Consuelo remembered the indecision of the teacher robot when the tumbleweed had stopped the hoverbus, and a slight feeling of hope surged in her that she might somehow escape.

The path was awash with water and was more like a stream. The rain continued to beat down and the fence of the dodo enclosure was beginning to buckle. The wall by the woolly mammoth was also crumbling, parts of it were being swept away. The woolly mammoth gave a loud bellow, its huge bulk stampeded towards them, as they stood motionless in fright. It rushed past them, nearly flattening Moon, who leaped desperately sideways, knocking over Consuelo as he did so. She picked herself up, mud and water dripping from her clothes and hair, and saw that the second robot seemed to have finally come to a decision. He pointed his gun at the three of them and said, "Carry on walking."

He marched behind, leaving his fellow soldier incapacitated on the ground, or pond, as it had now become. The group splashed slowly along and other animals appeared, taking refuge on walls or roofs. Consuelo stared at them, realising that not all were inmates of the zoo. They had been joined by refugees fleeing from the fire, who had evidently discovered a new source of food in the shape of the formerly extinct animals.

The auroch was being stalked by a cougar and it was apparent that it would only be a few seconds before the creature had once again become extinct. Squawks and bellows, muffled by the rain, came from every corner of the zoo, and it was very clear that the weaknesses which had originally caused their demise, were once again causing their downfall when attacked by a predator such as a cougar or bear.

The group paddled through the rising stream of the path and Consuelo saw that they had nearly reached the enclosure she and Logan had seen.

"I think he's taking us to the next cage," she whispered to Moon.

"No," he said, a frightened expression in his eyes. They reached the steel fence and Consuelo glanced to her left, trying to locate the Rio Grande. In her mind was the glimmer of an escape plan and she smiled in relief to see that it had left its meandering route and had flooded over the ground right up to the steel fence, which was still holding it at bay, its inner grounds waterlogged, but not swamped, by the turbulent river.

The robot turned his attention to the gate. He pressed a switch and it swung open. In that second, just as he glanced away, Consuelo sprang towards the river. She flung herself in, the cold biting at her, her mouth and nose filling with water. She could not swim, but had already decided it was better to risk drowning, than be imprisoned. She felt herself be taken by the strong current; she grabbed onto a large branch and in a few seconds had travelled some way down the river bank.

The water kept closing over her head, the current then pushing her back up to the surface again, and each time she reached the air, she gulped in as much as she could, to fill her lungs, before she was sucked under once more. She briefly glanced back at the robot and saw he was pursuing her along the bank, floundering and falling in the treacherous slime of the mud. He was firing his laser gun at her, and twice the water round her vibrated with its rays. She passed the bend of the river and he was lost to sight. She concentrated on staying alive in the churning rapids, managing to somehow stay afloat with her stout branch for at least two miles downstream from the zoo.

A copse of cottonwood trees was partly submerged in the river, and as the water swept her past it, she reached out and grabbed the root of a tree. It held her weight and she clung on, the current trying to snatch her from it. Then she slowly hauled herself along its twisted length and stumbled onto the waterlogged land.

She staggered through the trees to a higher part of the ground, and lay choking and gasping on the earth. She stayed there in exhaustion for a few minutes, before standing up with the help of a cottonwood trunk.

She knew the robots would be quickly on her track and could already hear the buzzing of a hoverwasp. She looked desperately about her, to see if there was any escape, and just as she had decided to go back into the

Rio Grande to put a greater distance between her, the zoo and Albuquerque, she recognised the picnic area she and the others had visited many years before.

It was difficult to find her bearings with all the water and the rain, and she stood quietly for a moment contemplating the terrain.

"That's it," she muttered, and slid down a bank towards an ungainly cactus she had suddenly recognised. She scrabbled frantically with her hands in the ground and uncovered a small hole in the bank.

She wriggled inside and found herself in the same large compartment she had discovered many years before. It was completely dark and she explored with her hands the four walls. She slumped onto the floor, uncaring about any insects and spiders which might be there, and rubbed her cold, wet arms to try and restore their circulation.

A faint murmur of hoverwasps sounded, but in the foetid, warm darkness she felt safe and gradually fell asleep in utter exhaustion.

Chapter 11

I want you to stay in the home pod today," RS752 had told Logan, as he and RS751 were on the point of going to their respective laboratories. "I have obtained an extension for you, as I said, but even so I think it is best for you to remain here."

Logan sat on his bed, worrying about his robot father's words. He bent down to touch the lizard, which was slowly investigating the corner of the room, sticking out its long tongue every so often, as though a juicy fly had appeared.

"Not much hope there, I'm afraid," Logan said to him. "I'll take you back to where you come from, when I can. But it won't be today, as there will be too many robots around."

He peered through the window at the rain beating against it and was startled to see a flash flood suddenly pour down the street. "Your society's so ordered, is it?" he muttered at the hoverbees and their occupants buzzing along. "But you can't control Nature, can you?"

He wandered round the living pod, unused to being on his own. RS751 had left him a haggis to eat and he poked at it with a fork. "What is this?" he said and took a few mouthfuls. "Yes, delicious," he declared and ate all of it.

He looked out of the window again and was pleased that the rain prevented him from seeing the Sandia Mountains. For a moment he thought he could see a bear amble round the corner, then disappear.

"My mind's playing tricks on me," he muttered and went to kick a ball in the corridor, an activity not usually allowed, as it disturbed RS752 in his study, which ran the whole length of the building, on the other side of the living pod.

He happily kicked the ball for about an hour, aiming it at one spot on the distant wall and attempting to perfect his technique. He dribbled it backwards and forwards. Then he became bored and was kicking it blindly anywhere, when he suddenly noticed that the door to RS752's study was ajar. He stared in surprise. It was forbidden territory and he had never been allowed inside before.

He stood curiously at the doorway, peering in. The room was grey and practically bare. A desk with a computer stood in the middle and boxes lined shelves. A door in the opposite wall led to other rooms and he walked over to it. He felt round the edge for an opening mechanism and it suddenly opened. He went back to the corridor and into the living pod, where he looked out of the window to see if his robot father's hoverbee was parked in the courtyard. There was no sign of it, or of any hoverbees belonging to the other residents in the building, and he rushed back to the study and entered the second room.

He blinked in surprise to see a bank of computer screens covering each wall from floor to ceiling. He stared at them, recognising his own living pod on one of them.

"What's this?" he muttered, turning his attention to the other screens which showed different living pods, although with no robot or human in them. He slowly glanced around the room, noticing that one screen had people in it. He went nearer, recognising the school classroom. The teaching robot appeared to be giving a lesson on thermodynamics, but the only pupil listening to it was Happy. The rest of the group were sitting at the back, clearly distressed. Violeta was crying, Poppy and Li were trying to comfort her, and Sky was sitting alone, a worried look on his face.

'What's happening? Where are the others? Where is Consuelo?" he muttered. His heart beat rapidly and he stared anxiously at the screen. He turned again to the living pods, trying to decide which one was Consuelo's, until he recognised her red dress with white spots, hanging on the back of a door.

"Where is she?" he muttered again. "It looks like all the sixteen-year olds, except for me, are not there. Is that why RS752 did not want me to go to school? Where have they taken them?"

"RS752 knows I have a hot temper, even if he can't understand it," he said to himself. "Perhaps he did not want me involved. I might have complicated things."

He stared in shock at the screens, his gaze flicking from one to the other. On the side wall were two more, and as he came nearer, he saw it was the enclosure he had seen at the zoo with Consuelo. The adjacent screen showed a room inside the building where Scorp and Moon were sitting glumly, then Scorp stood up and went to the window, which had bars on it. There was no sign of Consuelo, but Logan was more calm, thinking that it was probable she was with Scorp and Moon. He looked again at the bars, then at the enclosure outside, which was surrounded by the Rio Grande right up to the steel walls. On the gate a similar sign to those on the other cages was now attached. He peered at it and read the word, 'Human.'

He reeled in shock. "So that's our fate when we're sixteen," he muttered. "Our lives will end in imprisonment." He pounded the walls angrily with his fists. "How dare they?" he shouted. "How dare they?"

One more screen remained, which appeared empty. He glanced at it for a few seconds, puzzled because the room was filled with cuddly toys and dolls. A little face came into view, staring up at the camera. She was a very small human. Her hair was the colour of Logan's. It was dark chestnut and bobbed short. Her face was freckled and her eyes blue, the colour of starflowers. She was clutching a toy animal and dolls. Logan's heart stopped as he looked at her, instinctively knowing that she was related to him.

He stood transfixed. "She's alone," he murmured. "Where is she? She must be Honey, my replacement."

He gazed at her, then came to his senses and rummaged round the room to see if he could find anything that might be useful. He opened a cupboard door and saw two laser guns and a communication device. He looked at them briefly, before slamming the cupboard shut and going out of the rooms and back to his home pod.

Chapter 12

He rushed to his bed pod and began hastily packing his rucksack which smelled of smoke. He rummaged through the food dispenser for food and drink he could easily take with him, and discovered biscuits, cheese and a fizzy cola drink.

"I must find Consuelo," he muttered. "I should think she's somewhere in the zoo, even if she was not on the screen." He looked on his computer to locate the site and was cast down to see it was many miles away and would take him much of the day to walk there, even if he was not picked up by the robots before then. He glanced out of the window and saw that the rain had stopped.

"I'm not even sure she's there," he muttered, and reluctantly unpacked his rucksack and spent the rest of the day restlessly pacing the living pod, waiting to question RS752 and RS751 when they returned home.

He said nothing when they finally arrived, just sat playing with the lizard in his bed pod. The long day of anxiety had not reduced his anger at the discovery that he and the others had been continually spied on and that Consuelo had now been imprisoned, along with Scorp and Moon, and that would presumably also be his fate.

He kept his head down, saying nothing, his face as immobile as that of the robots. He sat at the table for dinner, trying to eat fish, chips and curry sauce, and switched on Robot News Today. The announcer did not begin with the usual account of orderly behaviour and robot achievements. Instead the Sandia Mountains appeared on the screen, blackened and with smoke rising from them. Logan grimaced, but continued to watch as the presenter announced, "There has been a small incident near Albuquerque, which has resulted in a forest fire. Our soldiers have now contained it. There are reports of wild animals fleeing the fire and moving into robot areas. These are also being dealt with. Another incident has been reported at the zoo in Albuquerque." The presenter stared into the camera, but said nothing more and went on to announce the completion of a train tunnel between New York and Moscow.

"What does he mean? A small incident at the zoo in Albuquerque?" said Logan.

"Yes," replied RS752.

"What did he mean?" asked Logan, in annoyance, pressing him to say more.

"I have bad news to tell you," RS752 said. "I think it will make you sad."

Logan's heart missed a beat. "What's that? What bad news?" he shouted, unable to contain himself any longer.

"Your fellow human, Consuelo, was swept away by the Rio Grande this morning. She is presumed dead. Some of her clothing has been found washed up on the river bank."

Logan stared wretchedly at RS752, suddenly realising why Consuelo had not been on the screen. Tears ran down his face and he sobbed uncontrollably. RS752 put his arm around him, but Logan pushed him away and ran into his bed pod where he lay on the floor, clutching the picture of Consuelo.

He passed the night, almost in a trance, devoured by his grief, but in the morning he changed his clothes, splashed water onto his face and was driven by RS752 to school. He was greeted by Violeta who rushed up to him. He picked her up, hugging her, and saw that her eyes were as red as his from crying.

"I want Consuelo. Where is she?" she cried.

Logan was unable to tell her the truth, so he remained silent and turned to Sky. "What happened yesterday?" he asked.

"I don't know," Sky replied. "We came in the morning and you, Consuelo, Scorp and Moon never arrived. The robots refused to tell us where you were and we thought you must all be together. Do you think they've been taken because they're sixteen?"

"I don't know. I was kept at home by my parents all day," said Logan grimly, unwilling to say anything about Consuelo, or the enclosure at the zoo, as it would be too distressing for the children.

The day passed slowly. Logan stared at the teacher, finding it difficult to conceal his hatred, his sadness overwhelming him. He no longer trusted any robot, his faith in RS752 shaken now that he had discovered his spying on the group. He remembered RS752's words, "I have obtained an extension for you," and the thought occurred to him that the robot families of Consuelo,

Scorp and Moon had not obtained extensions, and so they had been imprisoned.

"RS752 has protected me," he muttered. "Why has he behaved differently to the other robots?"

Chapter 13

Consuelo woke in a humid blackness which smelt of decay. For a moment she had no idea where she was, then the previous day's events rushed into her mind, making her shiver in fright. Her whole body ached and her limbs were so stiff it was difficult to move. There was earth in her nose and mouth and she spat it out. She slowly stood up and again felt round the room to discover more about her hiding place. The sides were not of earth, but of a more solid material, and appeared to have been built by someone. As her eyes became accustomed to the dark she distinguished a slight glimmer of light at one side. She stumbled towards it, curiously running her hand over the surface. It crumbled onto her feet and she choked in the dust it had released, which cleared, revealing the entrance to another room. She looked in and saw tree roots extending down to the floor and sunshine radiating into it from holes in the soil above.

She walked into the room, breathing in the somewhat fresher air more deeply, delighted to discover a less claustrophobic hiding place. She sat on the floor, her face turned to the sun, and gradually felt her strength and confidence return. She noticed a moss-covered table on which were a rusted tin and a dirt-encrusted doll, which lacked an arm. She picked them up and carried them back into her first refuge. Then she scrambled out through the hole and into the tree-shaded copse beyond, where she placed them on the ground next to her. She apprehensively looked at the river and the countryside, but nothing moved that resembled a robot or their vehicles. Pangs of hunger were making her nauseous and she desperately searched for something to eat. A pool of water lay in the crooked branch of a cottonwood and she gratefully cupped her hands and drank from it. She searched the copse, but the only food she could find were yellow berries from the barberry bush. She hesitated, for a moment staring at the green serrated leaves and bright yellow fruit, then picked several from the bush, eating them ravenously.

She sat down on the ground and let the heat of the day flow over her.

"If I return to Albuquerque I will be arrested and taken back to the zoo," she said to herself. "Perhaps I can walk to the mountains and live there alone. The robots don't seem to want to venture there." She sat pensively, her spirits sinking with the knowledge that it was almost impossible to escape undetected once she was in the open.

A shadow fell on the trees and she glanced up and saw in horror that turkey vultures were gathering above her and even at this distance she could distinguish their black wings with white and grey edges. She picked up a stone and threw it up through the trees, and although it reached nowhere near the birds, they moved away from her, coasting upwards on the air currents.

"I'm alive!" she called out loudly. "I'm not carrion yet!" and she jumped up and down, flapping her arms to prove her point, as well as frighten them away.

She sat back down on the dusty ground, watching the river flow by, which had now considerably receded from its flooded state and was meandering slowly again.

She glanced at a roadrunner which was dashing along the sandy bank in front of her. For a moment she was absorbed in watching the large bird with its distinctive crest. Then a rattling noise by a shrub made her jump in fright as a snake slithered into the undergrowth. In a flash she saw the diamond-shaped patterns along its back, and the black and white rings on its tail.

"A rattlesnake!" she cried out and ran in the same direction as the roadrunner until she found a flat patch of ground, hidden by the trees, where she could more easily see any predatory animal. She sat down once more and turned her attention to the tin and doll she had found underground.

The tin was rusted and had to be prised open by a sharp stone. Inside, she was surprised to find a necklace of pearls which gleamed when she held it up to the sunlight. She looked at it and caressed it with her fingers. Then she looked at the doll which she carefully wiped with a handful of dry lichen.

"These belonged to humans," she murmured. "Robots don't wear jewellery or play with dolls. Did humans make them, or did robots make them for humans, as they have for us?" She fastened the necklace round her neck and cradled the doll in her arms. She looked down at the Rio Grande, a chocolate colour once more, and at the dappled shadows on the dusty ground from the sun's rays filtering through the leaves.

"I am hunted, hungry and alone," she whispered. "But I am free."

Chapter 14

The following day, Logan jumped out of bed, his despair as black as the Sandia Mountains now were. He quickly dressed in clothes and shoes which would be suitable for walking the long distance to the zoo. He sat miserably eating a breakfast of rice and kippers, his second favourite after waffles and golden syrup, and switched on Robot News Today to see if there was any more news of the flooding and the invasion of wild animals into Albuquerque.

The screen showed scenes of terrible devastation in California. Buildings, roads and bridges had collapsed. Fires were raging, the flames spreading rapidly, engulfing whole streets.

"Tsunamis are at present roaring onto the coast," the presenter said, "and are rushing far inland. Thousands of robots are being swept out to sea. The whole of the west coast from Seattle in the north to San Diego in the south has been declared a disaster area and the force field for Sector 4 has been destroyed.

"What's happened?" Logan asked RS752, who had entered the pod and was watching the screen.

"There have been three simultaneous earthquakes in California, along the San Andreas and Hayward faults," he said and sat down with Logan to watch as the screen showed an arched bridge slowly collapsing into the water.

"That's the Golden Gate Bridge," remarked RS752.

Logan stared at the screen. "That's not like a normal bridge," he remarked. "It's curved."

"Yes," agreed RS752, somewhat reluctantly.

"Why is it different?" asked Logan.

"That's how it was made," hedged RS752, his shoulders almost imperceptibly shrugging.

Logan stared at the bridge again, then back at his robot father.

"It was made by humans," he suddenly guessed, his eyes wide with astonishment. "Humans made it," he repeated, the truth slowly dawning on him. "These names, 'Albuquerque', 'San Diego', 'San Francisco', 'Paris', 'Moscow', all of them. They're human names. Robots call everything by numbers or letters. They would not give names to places." He stopped for a moment, reflecting. "These human names are everywhere," he said. "They're all over P3, our planet. "There are hardly any robot names for places. I can only think of the four Sectors and P3.

He looked at RS752 and continued, "That's why you have given us names, not numbers like yourselves. It's because humans gave themselves names, as well as giving them to places."

He grabbed RS752's arms. "Tell me the truth," he said. "You owe it to me. You have created me and the others. You have used us in your experiment to see humans grow up, and you appear to be about to imprison us now that we are sixteen."

RS752 looked at him. "It is classified," he started to say, but Logan shouted over his words, and held on more tightly to RS752's metallic arms.

"Don't shout," said RS752. "I do not want other residents to hear that you are angry. It is possible they will call the soldiers."

Logan quietened down, his face flushed and angry.

"Let me go," said RS752 and Logan reluctantly stopped gripping his arms. "You are right," he said. "They are human names."

"They're everywhere!" said Logan in shock. "There must have been humans everywhere on the planet."

"Yes, that is correct," said RS752.

"What happened to them?" asked Logan.

"They died from a virus. They all died," replied RS752.

"How are we here then?" demanded Logan, but his robot father did not reply.

"So humans were once on P3, then became extinct," said Logan. "Like the dodo and the potoroo. So just as you have recreated those animals, you recreated humans, and now we're going to be put in a zoo, to be exhibited along with them."

He slumped onto a chair, hardly able to take in the horror of his own situation and the enormity of the realisation that the world had once teemed with humans.

"There were too many of them," said RS752. "They did not have enough food. They were very violent and always having wars. The planet has been saved by robots. We care for it and husband its resources. The planet nearly died because of humans and their pollution and their aggression."

"A tsunami is once more advancing onto the shore," said the presenter on Robot News Today and both RS752 and Logan turned to watch the wall of foaming water launch itself greedily over trees and buildings, smashing everything in its path.

"You cannot control everything," Logan said to RS752. "Nature is more powerful than robots."

"That is true," replied RS752, looking at Logan for a few seconds, then touching his arm. "I will keep asking for extensions for you," he said, "even when Honey is living here."

"I am just a specimen in an experiment to you?" queried Logan.

RS752 looked directly at him. "No, you are not," he said.

"Are you saying you have feelings?" asked Logan. "No robot has feelings."

"I am unique," replied RS752. "I was a prototype. My inventor created pathways in my circuitry to enable me to feel emotions slightly. I do not have the same feelings as a human, but I do have a certain amount of emotional output."

"I thought you were different," said Logan. "I was right. You do feel things."

"My body has been mended or replaced many times," replied RS752, "but I have always kept my original memory connections. It's so long ago that robots have forgotten about me, or else do not consider it important. It was decided that it was too dangerous to give feelings to robots, that it could lead to wars, even although we are far more intelligent than humans."

Logan looked at his robot father. "Does the human experiment finish at sixteen years because they are considered too aggressive when they get older?"

"That is one of the reasons," said RS752. "I have said too much. Do not say any of this to the other humans. It is classified and the consequences would be very serious for me."

"I will not say anything," said Logan, embracing his father.

At that moment, an army of hoverbuses could be heard advancing down the street. The droning noise was accompanied by the clatter of running feet and the sound of doors banging. Robot voices could be heard and Logan strode to the window to see what was happening.

"Most of the robots in Albuquerque have been allocated to repair the damage and help in the relief of California," RS752 said. "We are being taken in hoverbuses now."

"But you're not a worker robot," protested Logan.

"I am a scientist. I do not just deal with humans," RS752 replied. "I am needed to help repair the force field over Sector 4, so that we cannot come under attack."

"Attack by what?" enquired Logan.

"Meteors and space junk," replied RS752.

The red light started to flash on his communication device. "RS751 and I have to go now," he said. "Stay in the living pod until I return. It's safer for you at the moment."

He turned and left the pod. Logan peered down from the window and a few minutes later saw RS751 and

RS752 step into a hoverbus which boasted silver stripes along its length and appeared to take precedence over other hoverbuses as it flew up into the air and passed over the tops of the queue of vehicles.

Chapter 15

Logan waited in the living pod as hundreds of hoverbuses buzzed by in the street below, all going towards the west. Hour after hour they filed past, until by midday the road finally became deserted of traffic and robots, and a lone deer was the only occupant.

His mind was full of the revelation that there had once been humans on P3 and he strode backwards and forwards, the disaster on the news screen a backdrop to his thoughts.

Finally, when there was complete silence in the building and on the street, he went across the corridor and pressed the part of the wall that had a switch for RS752's study. He quickly glanced at the bank of screens and saw that the younger humans were in the classroom, and that Scorp and Moon were still captive. He went to the cupboard and took out the two laser guns and communication device, and stuffed them into his pocket.

Next, he rummaged through the food supply cabinet and packed fizzy drinks, biscuits and cheese into his rucksack and then ran down the stairs of his building and out into the courtyard, where a row of hoverbees stood parked. He chose RS752's and quickly climbed in.

It was not his first time driving it, RS752 had once let him have a go in the courtyard, but it seemed a very strange sensation to sit in the driving seat alone and manoeuver it out into the street. He scraped by the wall of the courtyard, jerking the vehicle up and down for a few yards, before managing to rise to a normal level and buzz slowly down the road.

Several miles later, he felt he was more in control, and very luckily had only met one other hoverbee along the whole route. He flew over the bridge of the Rio Grande and saw the zoo rapidly approaching in front of him. He buzzed over the steel entrance, following the same path he and Consuelo had taken a short time before. Most of the enclosures were empty of their inmates, and carcasses were everywhere, their bones picked clean by hundreds of turkey vultures which were congregating in large groups by the skeletons, or coasting up in the sky.

Logan shivered as he saw the almost featherless birds, with their pink, wrinkled heads and huge, black wings tipped with white or grey.

"You're not eating me!" he shouted at one which soared down directly in front of the hoverbee, causing him to pull up sharply to avoid a collision.

He reached the last compound, near the Rio Grande, and buzzed over it twice to see if there was any robot in the vicinity, but there appeared to be no guard, unless he was inside the building.

He decided to take a chance and parked the hoverbee just outside the front entrance. He climbed out and pushed against the door, but it was locked. He ran round to the side and discovered barred windows, similar to those he had seen on the screen. He peered through the glass and saw Moon and Scorp sitting in front of a screen watching the news.

"Hey!" he called, banging on the glass between the bars. They turned round and saw him and ran to the window.

"Help us!" called Moon. "Let us out. They've imprisoned us."

"What's happened to Consuelo?" cried Logan.

"She jumped in the river and escaped," said Moon.

"Do you know if she survived?" asked Logan, his heart beating rapidly.

"I don't know. The soldier was shooting at her, but she reached the bend in the river and was holding onto a branch," Scorp replied. "The soldier ran back to lock us in and there was no sign of Consuelo."

"So she might be alive," Logan said, having difficulty speaking.

"Yes, it's possible, but I should think they would soon find her. There's nowhere to hide," Scorp replied unhappily.

"I must go and look for her before I'm caught" said Logan. "I will come back for you when I have found somewhere you can hide and where we can go." He raced back to the hoverbee, jumped in and buzzed away before a robot appeared.

He buzzed slowly along the bank of the Rio Grande, searching for any sign of human clothing. The ground was still either flooded or very waterlogged, and trees were often submerged up to their lower branches.

Turkey vultures were sitting on many of them, whilst snakes were coiled round others. He accelerated, hovering dangerously over bushes and cacti and swerving between trees. He recognised the copse of cottonwoods where they had picnicked several years before, and landed the hoverbee on an open patch of dry, sandy ground which had escaped the flooding.

He clambered out and wandered through the cottonwoods and mesquite. A roadrunner ran past him and he smiled, as he always did, on seeing the large brown bird shoot along, its crest waving.

He sat on a bank and looked down the river. There was another copse of cottonwood, juniper and mesquite, on the bank of the next meander, but after that there was nothing but poor scrubland with stunted bushes and cacti.

He grimaced and glanced round the copse, seeing nothing to suggest Consuelo had been there. He looked up and saw the turkey vultures gathering in the sky, almost directly above him, and he fearfully searched the area for a body. There seemed no obvious reason for them to be congregating, and he looked more carefully again by the trees. There was no smell of carrion, only the fresh scent of juniper. He idly picked a yellow berry from a barberry bush and stubbed his toe against a metal box.

He picked it up in surprise. "Perhaps we left it here all those years ago," he muttered.

He suddenly recalled Consuelo falling into a hole, and glanced around to see where it might be, the thought occurring to him that it was the only hiding place to be found. He noticed the odd, angular shape of the forked cactus and it came into his mind that the hole was somewhere near it. He carefully scrutinised the bank and saw that the soil had been moved. He scrabbled in the earth and uncovered the entrance to the hole, a slight noise from inside making him wary, in case it was a coyote or a cougar. He waited to see if any animal rushed out, or made a sound, but there was nothing and all he could hear was a roadrunner cooing near the river.

"It's me, Logan," he called out, not expecting any response.

The next minute, Consuelo came tumbling out of the hole. She stood up, her clothes dishevelled, her hair matted and dirty, and her face smeared with earth.

"Oh Logan," she cried tearfully, throwing herself into his arms. They embraced and Consuelo clung to him as though she thought he would abandon her at any moment.

"Don't worry, I'm here," he said, holding her tightly.

"How did you find me?" Consuelo asked.

"I don't know," he cried. "I came down the river in the hoverbee and I was just looking everywhere. I didn't really expect to find you. RS752 said you had drowned."

"I nearly did," she cried, sobbing and laughing at the same time. I was so frightened in the water, but I did not want to be imprisoned. It was my last chance to save myself. I would prefer to die than to spend the rest of my life in a cage at the zoo."

"Yes," agreed Logan. "You're right. I would prefer to have a few days of freedom than a life of captivity."

"Have you stolen the hoverbee?" she asked. "Surely they must be after you as well?"

"No," he replied. "Most of the robots have left Albuquerque and gone to California, which has been devastated by earthquakes and tsunamis."

"What am I going to do?" asked Consuelo. "I'm so hungry,"

"I've brought some food," Logan said and went over to the hoverbee, where he produced the provisions he had brought.

Consuelo ate and drank ravenously, then lay back exhausted.

"I think I know where you can hide," he said. "I don't know when the robots will return, so it's best not to stay in my living pod. Lie down on the floor of the hoverbee so that you can't be seen and I'll take you there. If a robot sees me, it's not as bad as if they see you."

Consuelo squeezed into the back and crouched on the floor, and Logan raised the vehicle into the air and accelerated, crossing the Rio Grande without using the bridge.

He drove carefully, following the maze of streets on the far side of Albuquerque. He drove past the Human History Archives building, halting just outside the entrance to the alley.

"Quick! Get out! This is the place," he said to Consuelo, and they both swiftly left the vehicle. "In here," he said, pulling her between the giant cactus and into the quiet street beyond.

"What's this?" she asked.

"It's an old human house," Logan replied. "They think you've drowned, so they won't be looking for you anywhere."

He led her through the gap in the wall and into the ruined room beyond, and they stood together staring up at the pinyon pine and at a hummingbird darting from flower to flower.

"It's so beautiful," said Consuelo, and burst into tears again.

"Don't cry," said Logan, putting his arms round her. "I'll go home and get things for you."

He took out the laser gun from his pocket. "Take this," he said. "Press this button to use it if anything threatens you. It will stop a robot, or kill a rattlesnake. If you need to use it to defend yourself, then do so." With that, he hugged her again, then ran back to the hoverbee and quickly drove home.

Chapter 16

He drove the hoverbee recklessly through deserted streets and by the time he returned home, it was not in quite the same condition as before, having crashed into a wall and dented its side panel. He lowered it down onto the courtyard and raced up the stairs. He grabbed more food and drink, sleeping bags, a plastic covering, a torch and the lizard, and dashed back down to the hoverbee. He drove more carefully this time, not wanting to attract attention, and parked the vehicle a few streets from the alley. He hurriedly strode along the sidewalk, watching out for robots. Then he looked in each direction before squeezing between the cactus into the welcoming dark of the alley. Consuelo greeted him, holding onto him as though she would never let him go, and they sat quietly on the ground, gazing at each other in delight.

"I'll stay here tonight with you. I'm sure they won't be back today. They've only just left," said Logan.

"I've kept secrets from you," he continued guiltily. "I didn't want to, but it was necessary. I wanted to protect you and the group. The day that the soldiers came to the school, I found a building near here which has a sign on it saying Human History Archives. I've got to go and see what's there. I also discovered today fromRS752 that there used to be many humans living here on this planet and they all died from a virus."

"Shall we go to the Human History Archives tonight?" asked Consuelo. "We don't know how long it will be before the robots return."

"No, you must stay here," Logan said. "It might be dangerous."

"I'm sure it's not more dangerous than leaping into the river and being fired on by a soldier," replied Consuelo "I don't care. We have to discover as much as we can. There's so few of us and at the moment we don't seem to have a future. We owe it to the younger ones to try and find out where we come from, even if we die."

She happily watched the hummingbird as it hovered, its rainbow colours catching the last rays of the sun. She held out her hand to Logan. "Come on, it's time to go," she said, smiling at him.

The sun was setting as they emerged from the alley. Night was rapidly blackening the sky as Logan peered out cautiously along the street, before running to the hoverbee. Consuelo hid in the back and Logan drove it rapidly to the Human History Archives building. He accelerated and made the vehicle rise higher into the air, passing over the wall into the deserted compound, with tattered shreds of paper littering the weed-choked ground. He hovered briefly to see if there was a robot and then put it down. There were no lights in the building, which still had part of its roof missing.

"It doesn't look as though any robots come here much," remarked Consuelo, as she climbed out of the hoverbee.

"There were robot workers here the day of the storm," said Logan. "We mustn't take it for granted that a robot won't appear."

He pushed the front door which creaked as it swung open, and they stepped together into a square hall, looked down on by the night sky. Puddles of water gathered on a cracked floor and a brown snake slunk evasively into a side room. Consuelo and Logan wandered cautiously along a corridor leading off from the main hall, glancing into rooms which contained ancient, rusted machinery in a variety of odd shapes and sizes.

Consuelo stopped to look at an object which had an elongated barrel attached to a handle. "What's this?" she said, picking it up and touching the trigger. "It's a bit like a laser gun, but it's not rectangular." She pulled back the trigger, whereupon it gave a loud bang and a metal bullet ricocheted off a tin bowl and into a door.

She shrieked, then put her hand to her mouth, drawing in her breath. "I'm sorry," she said. "It could have killed us."

"This place could be a death trap," said Logan and they wandered even more carefully through the rooms, not handling anything.

They reached the only part of the building which possessed a roof. The objects in the room appeared to be of more recent origin than the previous ones they had seen. They stopped to look closely and saw directly in front of them, on the wall, a modern computer screen.

"This isn't from the past," said Logan. "It's like the one at home. He settled on a chair in front of it and typed the words, 'The History of Humans' on the keyboard, and immediately the screen lit up.

"I hope the robots can't see the glow," said Consuelo. "It's very bright."

"We'll have to risk it," said Logan.

They sat together, holding each other's hands, as images of humans appeared, and for the first time in sixteen years they discovered their human ancestry on P3, whose name was originally Earth.

Hours passed. They saw images of early man and the cave paintings at Lascaux. They saw Stonehenge and the Coliseum and the Parthenon. They saw a picture of the Trojan Horse, filled with soldiers to enter Troy and destroy it. They laughed at pictures of people dressed in the most peculiar clothing, some with only loin cloths and bones in their noses, others in beautiful, silk dresses padded out at the back as though the wearers had enormous bottoms. Some images saddened them and made them cry. Many wars had happened. Primitive weapons such as swords and axes were used to hurt and kill other humans, and in a later century, they saw the atomic bombs on Hiroshima and Nagasaki; the destruction of much of Europe and concentration camps where people huddled, starving, in striped garments.

They saw also centuries of art and culture, Leonardo da Vinci's paintings, including the Mona Lisa which Logan recognised from his bed pod, and other art which featured a cow in a tank of formaldehyde.

"That's very strange," remarked Consuelo.

Their brains reeled from so much information in such a short time, and as the dawn broke, they sat, emotionally and physically exhausted, and finally discovered music. The strains of 'Robin Hood, Robin Hood riding through the glen, Robin Hood, Robin Hood, with his band of men,' filled the room, followed by 'Davy, Davy Crocket, king of the wild frontier.' Their feet tapped and they started singing with the words, and Consuelo jumped up and danced to the beat.

Then they heard Beethoven's 1812 overture and sat entranced, smiling at each other.

"Humans are not just violent, as RS752 said. They had wars and did terrible things to each other, but they were creative and often kind. They were a mixture of so many different and wonderful things," said Consuelo.

They saw the creation of robots and how their intelligence quickly surpassed that of their creators. Soon robots appeared in human armies and governments and everywhere which was essential to the whole fabric of human society and the organisation of the planet. They saw humans speaking out about the dominant role which had been given to robots and expressing their unease. They saw that robots had been vital in space travel and had helped to explore the planets in the solar system and to create an atmosphere on Mars, where a colony was established.

"Humans visited Mars," exclaimed Logan. "They didn't just stay here on P3."

Then, finally, they discovered the extinction of humans. A virus had swept across the world, killing everyone. Consuelo and Logan were unable to watch the horrible scenes and fast-forwarded the machine. Robots were seen cleaning up the polluted Earth and constructing a stable and peaceful society.

"How are robots making us?" Logan said. "We need to know. I think we're cloned. I'm sure that's how they have made woolly mammoths and all the other extinct animals."

He typed in the words, 'Human Baby Factory.' "RS752 said that's where we come from."

The screen showed a large, white building near the river. He typed in the name 'Logan' and a picture came up of him as a young child.

"You look very sweet," laughed Consuelo, her fright slightly evaporating.

He then asked the computer for a list of people who had been used in the cloning process and he and Consuelo were startled to see names appear, as well as images. First was Consuelo Lopez. She had snow-white hair and dark brown eyes and was standing in front of a gathering of soberly dressed humans. "The last President of the United States of America,' Logan read out.

"That's me when I'm old," muttered Consuelo unhappily.

"I don't know what a President was or the United States of America," said Logan, "but you look important."

Next came Colonel Steve McIntyre, who was a scientist and an astronaut and led the first mission to colonise Mars. He too looked old. His hair was also white and he looked out from the screen with eyes the colour of starflowers. "That's me," muttered Logan. "Me and Honey." He had also invented the first robot to have some sort of feeling. "He invented RS752," exclaimed Logan.

Li was cloned from another President, whose name was Li Wan Phong, this time from a place called China; Violeta was cloned from the last commander of the Earth's Army, Moon from an artist called Abdul Sheikh; Star from a musician called Bappy Rat; Poppy from a film star called Dolores Moppet; Sky from a man called Lemuel Mackintosh, a scientist; Rosa from a doctor, Henriette Champignon, and the young Honey from Isabella McIntyre who was also an astronaut and scientist, like her brother Steve.

"What's a film star?" wondered Consuelo.

"I have no idea," replied Logan.

Finally, Scorp came from an ugly man with a very large nose and close-set eyes, called Rafe Baumgartner, who had been a war criminal from Venezuela.

"That doesn't surprise me," remarked Logan sourly.

"What about Happy?" remarked Consuelo. "He's not there."

"No, he's not. That's strange," Logan said. They all sound important in human society and they're all different. They've chosen a cross-section of humans."

"I think we'll go now," said Consuelo wearily. "It's too much for me. I'm not sure I want to be a clone of someone and I don't wish to see how I'll look when I'm old. Although it doesn't seem very likely that I'll ever get to be old with things how they are at the moment."

"Is there anything about the group experiment, apart from how we were made?" she questioned. "After all, we are part of human history, even if there are only nine of us."

"Ten," corrected Logan. "There's also Honey."

"It's not right that she's only with robots," Consuelo said. "She needs to be with other humans and to be properly cared for."

"Yes," agreed Logan, typing in the words, 'Human Experiment conducted by robots.' A picture of the whole group filled the screen. "We are here," he muttered in amazement. "They've stuck us at the end of human history."

He and Consuelo stared at each other and then at the screen, reading the words.

'Robot scientists are currently conducting an experiment to observe human behaviour as they grow, within robot society. At sixteen they are considered to be adult and in view of the previous record of human aggression, they will be confined for the rest of their lives at the zoo, where their behaviour can be observed, along with other animals.'

Consuelo and Logan looked at each other in shock.

"They're not going to confine me!" Consuelo declared. "I would sooner be dead."

At that moment a noise sounded in the corridor. They both jumped up, frightened. "Let's hide," said Logan and they gazed desperately round the bare room.

"There's nowhere," muttered Consuelo. "We'll be captured."

Logan took out the laser gun. "Stand behind me," he said, and as Consuelo did so, a robot soldier entered. "What are you doing?" he said. "This is a restricted area. Are you the one who is missing?" he said, looking at Consuelo.

Logan and Consuelo had no response to make. Their hoverbee was outside and it was quite apparent who they were and what they were doing.

The soldier's hand moved towards his laser gun, but Logan was quicker and fired at the soldier, who fell shuddering to the floor.

"You've killed him," shrieked Consuelo.

"Destroyed, not killed," Logan replied. "He's not human."

They stared in anguish at the metallic corpse.

"What shall we do?" said Consuelo.

"Let's put him in that box," replied Logan, going over to the robot and picking up his legs. Consuelo took his shoulders and together they deposited him in the metal container and shut the lid.

"He's surprisingly light," remarked Consuelo.

"Yes, "agreed Logan. "It was him or us. I had no choice."

"Yes, you were completely right," agreed Consuelo.

"Let's go now," she said, her voice trembling. Other robots might come."

"No, there's two more things I need to discover," said Logan. "Humans evidently went to the planets and created an atmosphere on Mars. Perhaps they're living there now?"

"The virus is bound to have killed them as well. They would not have existed without contact with their home planet," said Consuelo.

Logan stayed quiet for a few seconds, thinking.

"Do you remember that pink explosion I showed you on the moon. That wasn't normal. It seemed strange. It's possible there are humans still there," he exclaimed.

"I want to go. I'm afraid," said Consuelo.

Logan hugged her and said, "We've got to know if there are any other humans out there." He typed, 'Humans on the Moon' and was gratified to see pictures of enormous bubbles, next to which were ancient rockets. Nothing more came on the screen and he tried, 'Humans on Mars'. This time images of Mars showed the red soil of the planet dotted with a variety of irregularly-shaped buildings.

"Those are human," said Logan. "The robots wouldn't build anything that wasn't square or rectangular." Other images flickered onto the screen, showing trees, flowers and grass.

"It's obvious humans did live there with an atmosphere," said Consuelo. "It's whether they are still there now."

She and Logan quietly left the Human Archives building, failing to notice the camera eye swivelling to watch them over the front door, and buzzed back in the hoverbee to its previous parking place. The streets were completely deserted and day was dawning.

"It's odd that there's no robot around at all," Logan remarked, as he and Consuelo ate breakfast in the shade of the pinyon pine.

"Except for…" and she nodded in the direction of the Human History Archives building.

"Yes, except for him," he muttered reluctantly.

"It's our home," said Consuelo proudly, looking around her at the flowers and cacti.

"Yes, it's ours," agreed Logan.

Then they fell asleep, Consuelo's head on Logan's shoulder, overwhelmed and exhausted by what they had seen.

Chapter 17

"I have to go home," he told Consuelo when they both woke to the warmth of the early morning sun. "The computer there is very powerful because of the scientific research that my robot parents do. I know that RS752 communicates with satellites high up above P3. I will try and send a signal to the Moon. I realise it's unlikely to be received, or that there will be a human there, but I have to try."

He left Consuelo fast asleep again in her sleeping bag under the pinyon pine, the lizard scuttling round on the stones near her, and placed the laser gun by her hand.

He drove rapidly in the hoverbee, enjoying the sensation of manoeuvring the small vehicle, and marvelling again at the lack of robots on the streets. "California must be terribly devastated," he muttered to himself.

He parked the hoverbee in the courtyard and ran up the stairs, pleased to return to the familiarity of his home pod, although anxious about having left Consuelo. He sat down at the computer and adjusted the settings to communicate with the satellites. He had seen RS752 do it many times before and knew it was not complicated. He increased the power of the signal he was sending and adjusted the setting again to coincide with the orbit of the Moon.

"It's lucky I've had a good robot education," he muttered.

The screen flickered. There was interference. There seemed to be voices talking in the background which he dismissed as wishful thinking.

Then he nearly collapsed with shock. A young man who had black hair and eyes and a similar olive skin to Consuelo, and who was wearing a grey uniform, appeared on the screen. Logan stared at him for a moment, words failing him. The stranger stared back at him, his eyes bemused.

"Where are you calling from?" he asked. "The signal seems to be coming from Earth.

"It is Earth," Logan managed to splutter, remembering that was the name of P3. "I am Logan. I'm a human."

"I can see you're a human," said the man, a slight smile on his face. "Why shouldn't you be? However, I don't think you're communicating from Earth, as all humans are dead there. The signal must be faulty, or else you're playing a practical joke. I'm afraid I haven't got any time to waste, I'm busy," and the picture disappeared from the screen.

Logan sent the signal again with quivering fingers.

The man reappeared. "It's you again. I told you I'm busy," and he moved his hand as though to switch off the communication again.

"No, don't go," cried Logan desperately. "I am really calling from Earth. I am in a group which is part of an experiment to see the behaviour of humans as they grow. We've all been cloned."

The man stared at him. "Wait," he said, "I'll get Colonel Tolstoy." He jumped up and disappeared from the screen, allowing Logan to see a window in the room, on the other side of which was a rough terrain of rocks. Another man then appeared, also dressed in grey, and the two men stared at Logan, without speaking, for some seconds.

"We need help," Logan said. "We're going to be imprisoned in cages at the zoo for the rest of our lives. They have finished their experiment with two of us, and they are already captive there. We all need to leave P3, I mean Earth," he corrected himself. "Is it possible for you to come and rescue us?"

The two men continued to stare at him and Logan noticed an ungainly vehicle whizz past the window, churning up dust from the lunar surface which was in extremely bright sunlight.

"Tell me where you are exactly," said the Colonel.

"We're all in Albuquerque, in Sector 4," Logan replied.

"Is that Albuquerque in New Mexico?" asked the man.

"I've never heard of New Mexico, but it's definitely Albuquerque. It's near the Sandia Mountains and the Rio Grande river," Logan said, adding, "I'm cloned from a human who was called Steve McIntyre."

The men stared at him in amazement. " Yes," said the Colonel. "Yes," he said slowly. "He died long ago but I've seen pictures of him and yes you do look like him." He stared hard at Logan. "I'm very sorry," he said, "but it's impossible to rescue you. We have our shuttle rocket here at the moment which goes regularly to Mars, but we can't penetrate the force field of Earth. The robots' defence system is extremely strong."

"It's not working in our Sector at the moment, which is Sector 4" said Logan. "There's been a terrible earthquake in California and it is being repaired."

"Is that right? We did not know," replied the man. "Let me check," and he went over to another computer screen.

"Yes," he returned to say. "Yes, you're right. There isn't a force field at the moment."

"I don't know when it will be restored," said Logan. "Can you come soon?"

"The shuttle rocket is being prepared for the Mars voyage," the Colonel said, "and is nearly ready to blast off, so we can use that. We will need to land somewhere flat and smooth. Do you know the White Sands area?"

"Yes," said Logan, "but it's some distance from here. I think we can reach it by morning. Is that acceptable to you?"

"Yes," said the Colonel. "How many are there of you?"

"Nine," said Logan, then corrected himself, remembering Honey "No, ten."

"We can manage to fit in ten of you," said Colonel Tolstoy. "We will not want to delay very long on Earth. We will descend very rapidly through the Earth's atmosphere, stop briefly to pick you up and leave. The robots will attack us if they can."

"I thought they were not aggressive," said Logan.

The man laughed. "They killed all humans on Earth by infecting them with a virus and then took over our planet. Not aggressive!" and he laughed again.

Logan was so shocked he could hardly speak and just stared at the screen.

"If you are not there, we will go without you," said Colonel Tolstoy. "It's a great risk for us to come, as we do not have many space shuttles and we need them. However, we are looking forward to meeting you and the others very much and we will do our best to rescue you. Can we check the time with you? We will rendezvous at zero ten hours Earth time at the northernmost point of White Sands."

"Yes. I understand," said Logan. "Zero ten hours at White Sands. Thank you."

"Goodbye," said the Colonel.

Logan turned off the signal, hoping that it had not been intercepted by the robots. He then picked up a communication device and pressed the red button to speak to RS752 who answered immediately. "Is that you Logan? Are you alright?"

"Yes, Dad," he replied. "I'm just communicating with you to see what's happening with the earthquake."

"It's not too good," replied RS752.

"What about the force field, Dad? Is it still not working?"

"Yes, it is still not working," replied his robot father. "It will not be repaired for several days."

"Goodbye, Dad," said Logan, his voice breaking slightly. "Goodbye."

"Goodbye, my son," said RS752. "Whatever the future brings I have faith in your ability to deal with it. I do not command the experiment, although I have a senior position, and I want you to understand I do not always agree with the decisions that are made. Goodbye."

The communication device went silent and Logan wiped a tear from his eye as he realised he would never see his robot father again. Then he rushed rapidly down the stairs and into the hoverbee, where his excitement made him hit the wall as he left the courtyard, and graze the surface of a further two on the way, all the time singing, "Davy, Davy Crocket, King of the wild frontier," at the top of his voice, as he drove back to the alley and the ruined house.

Chapter 18

"There are humans on the Moon and Mars!" he shouted, rushing into the ancient, ruined house.

Consuelo stared at him in amazement. "Humans on the Moon and Mars!" she exclaimed.

"Yes, he said. "I spoke to two of them on the computer screen at home. They're sending something called a Space Shuttle to try and rescue us tomorrow."

"Tomorrow?" she repeated in bewilderment.

"Yes. We've got to go to White Sands, which is a long way to the south of Albuquerque, and they will pick us up there."

Consuelo stood and stared, hardly able to take it in. She swayed and dropped to the ground, Logan catching her as she fell.

"Sit down, you're exhausted," he said. He gave her the fizzy drink of cola and a biscuit and she quickly recovered, her face still very pale and black shadows under her eyes.

"We've got to find all the others and set off to White Sands," he said. I'll need to steal a hoverbus. It's large enough for everyone and it's also quick and will get us there in time."

"Stop, Logan!" cried Consuelo. "Don't talk like this. You can't possibly steal a hoverbus. I expect they've all gone to California."

"Well, I'm going to try," said Logan determinedly. I've been to the workshop before with RS752, where they make them. There might be one or two there that have not been taken to California. If we can't get a hoverbus, it's easy to find hoverbees as their owners have all gone. The problem is that some of the others will have to drive them and they've never done so before."

He and Consuelo rapidly packed up the sleeping bags and torch as well as the remainder of the food. Consuelo looked around her sadly at the honeysuckle blooms with their attendant hummingbird, and then stepped through the crack in the wall and into the alley. Logan looked at the lizard, "Goodbye Lizzie. You're home again now, just as I might be home with other humans soon." He softly touched its dry skin. Then he joined Consuelo.

Logan tried to keep his excitement from clouding his judgement. He peered out of the alley as cautiously as usual, before running swiftly to the hoverbee and driving it back to Consuelo, to minimise the risk of her being seen. She jumped and hid in the back, as before, and he turned the vehicle in the street and drove at a moderate speed so as not to arouse suspicion. It was not difficult to find the building, which lay only a short distance away and he hovered above its yard.

"Look, there's two over there," pointed out Consuelo. "Do you think they're working? We don't want to break down."

A robot came out of the workshop and glanced up at the circling hoverbee. He stared at it briefly, picked up a tool from the ground, then went back inside the building. Logan quickly set down the hoverbee next to the hoverbus which was furthest from the workshop.

"Hurry, get out," he said to Consuelo. "Let's do it!" He gave her the laser gun, "You have it. I'll need both hands free to drive."

She held it in her hands, her expression determined, and Logan jumped into the driving seat of the hoverbus, started the energy box and accelerated, rising up steeply into the air and zooming out of the yard.

"We'll go to the school first and see if we can take the children," Logan said. "It's nearly time for lunch and they will all be together without a robot teacher. He parked the hoverbee just outside the school gates and left Consuelo lying down in the back so as not to be seen.

He raced into the school and found everyone eating at the dining table, as he had expected. Their faces turned towards him and Violeta ran up to him as usual and gave him a hug.

"You've all got to come with me," he said. "I can't explain now, but it's very important and you will see Consuelo. Happy immediately jumped up and grabbed his bag from the back of his chair. "Yes, we'll come," he said. The others were less sure, looking down at their unfinished dinners of roast beef and Yorkshire pudding, but Logan picked up Violeta and Poppy. "Come on," he said. "It will be an adventure."

Everyone quickly followed him out of the building to the waiting hoverbus and they all jumped in, delighted to find Consuelo on the floor.

"Sh," she whispered. "Wait until we're moving to greet me." Logan looked back at the school and thought he saw a robot at the school window, but he did not pursue them, and Logan wondered if he had perhaps not noticed their departure.

He drove as quickly as he could to the Rio Grande, the others chattering excitedly as Consuelo explained what they were doing. He passed the river and buzzed into the zoo, parking just outside the human prison buildings. He picked up the laser gun and looked around to see if there were robots. Again, there were none and he fired the laser gun at the door, destroying the lock. It gave way and he ran into the room where he had seen Mars and Moon, and found them both slumped in front of the news screen in a similar fashion to the last time he had seen them.

"Quick!" he shouted. "You've got to escape now. I've found a place for us to go."

They did not hesitate or ask questions. They just stood up and ran with him out to the hoverbus and jumped in.

There was one more place Logan had to visit and he drove as fast as he could. He passed a few hoverbees, but no one seemed to notice them and no sirens sounded, and as he drove, Consuelo explained to the others what was happening and where they were going.

Logan parked outside the Human Baby Factory and looked around for robots. Two were walking away down the street and as he ran into the building he noticed another two walking up the stairs. He had no idea where to go and rushed desperately from one floor to another, peering in all the rooms. Finally, he noticed a door with a picture of a bee and a pot of honey on it and pushed it open, his heart in his mouth, in case he was confronted by robots.

Instead, all by herself, sat Honey in a metal playpen. She glanced at him, stood up and held out her arms, smiling solemnly. He picked her up, gave her a big kiss, then ran down the stairs and out of the building and into the hoverbus.

He revved the energy box and they raced through the streets, crossed the Rio Grande and headed south.

Chapter 19

Logan drove steadily towards White Sands, following the highway south. Angular, spiky bodies of cacti rose up repeatedly, like sentinels, in the dusty terrain around them. Some were enormous, standing in strange, distorted shapes, dwarfing the other spindly shrubs and trees. Logan looked constantly behind them for any sign of pursuit but could see nothing. Only a few vultures marred the sky, not the squadron of hoverhornets he was expecting.

Bird and animal life, on the contrary, abounded. Slender roadrunners were darting over the highway and scrubland below them, their crests bobbing. A rabbit was hopping along, stalked silently by a cougar, which looked strangely out of place in the desert-like environment.

"Another refugee from the Sandia Mountains," said Logan, pointing it out to Sky. "It's escaped capture by the robots, just like we have."

"We hope," muttered Sky.

A rattlesnake was coiled on top of a flat bush, sunning itself, its grey-brown skin and diamond markings on its back blending in with the twigs and leaves.

At times, the dusty scrubland became short grass prairie, speckled with flowers of scarlet globe-mallow, thread-leaf groundsel and yellow-spine thistle; the occasional tree of pinyon pine, gambel oak, brown snakeweed and one-seed juniper, giving shade from the burning heat of the day. In the air were golden eagles and hawks, and as they continued further south, flocks of black vultures could be seen congregating in huge, seething masses on the ground, as well as coasting up and down on air currents, frightening the children.

A slight wind was catching balls of tumbleweed, blowing them across the countryside, and Logan kept the hoverbus high in the air to avoid a breakdown like that near the zoo on the bridge over the Rio Grande. Consuelo taught everyone the Davy Crocket and Robin Hood songs and they kept singing the same two tunes for hours, entranced by the new sensation of music, with the exception of Happy, who said he was not able to sing. However, he sat cheerfully listening to the others and drumming his fingers on the seat. Logan glanced round at Consuelo as she led the singing for about the hundredth time and she smiled back at him anxiously.

After several hours, his eyes started to close in exhaustion.

"Let me drive," said Scorp. "You're going to have an accident."

"No," said Logan, although hesitating for a moment. "We will stop here for a short break," and brought the vehicle down onto a patch of open ground, near to a rocky outcrop colonised by a tangle of cacti, their prickly arms ranged at odd angles, and interweaving with each other.

Scorp scowled at Logan and went to sit at the back of the hoverbus again with his friends, Happy and Poppy. Logan clambered stiffly down onto the ground and glanced at the sky, where only a few cirrus clouds marred its vivid blue, not a squadron of hoverhornets.

"They're not pursuing us," he said in relief. "It's strange though," he muttered, shaking his head.

"Don't worry," said Consuelo, the expression on her face as concerned as his. "You're doing wonderfully. Just concentrate on getting us to White Sands."

She wandered to the other side of the knoll, where a gully cut into the scrubland. Stones littered the ground, washed down from a scree by a flash flood, and the remains of a green, stagnant pool were watched over by a dead willow tree and the bleached bones of an animal. Consuelo shivered.

"It's an omen," remarked Poppy. "I want to go back to my parents. I don't want to go to the moon." Her blue eyes were tearful in her pale face and her long, fair hair hung limply in the heat.

"We can't leave you behind," said Sky. "You would be completely alone, without any other humans. You would spend the rest of your life in an enclosure at the zoo, looked at by robots as though you are some sort of animal."

"You've got to come with us," said Consuelo. "We can't abandon you."

Poppy collapsed sobbing onto a rock and Consuelo put her arms round her.

Honey toddled across the sandy ground, chasing a ball of tumbleweed, followed by Violeta, their laughter echoing up through the walls of the gully, disturbing black ravens which flew off, cawing loudly. Logan looked around him uneasily.

"We'll just stop a short time," he said, glancing again at the horizon, where a dark line was just becoming visible and a faint drone could be heard.

"What's that?" he exclaimed and ran quickly to the hoverbus, which he climbed into, rapidly raising it into the air and putting it back down in the gully, underneath the dead trees.

"It's more difficult to see it now," he said, as he opened the door and jumped out. "Everyone come over here and hide by this scree."

"I think that's a cave," shouted Moon, pointing to a dark opening high up in the rock. "Let's go up there."

They scrabbled up the slippery scree towards the hole, Consuelo helping Violeta, and Logan carrying Honey. He peered in cautiously. It was as black as the night, and a smell of rotting flesh emanated from it. He drew the laser gun from his pocket, gave Honey to Consuelo and scrambled in first. The small entrance opened up into a much larger cave and Logan quickly pulled everyone inside.

They sat there, on the sand and rocks, holding hands in the darkness.

"Happy and Scorp aren't here!" Logan looked round and suddenly exclaimed. "Where are they?"

"I saw them both go up to the cacti on top of the hill," volunteered Sky. "I think they must still be there."

"I'll go and get them," muttered Logan unhappily, peering out from the cave and staring into the distance at the approaching hoverhornets. "They'll be seen amongst the cactus! It's much safer to be here!"

He threw himself headlong down the slope, grazing his face and hands and ripping his clothes. He ran out of the gully and up the sides of the knoll and into the outstretched arms of the cacti. The sharp spikes tore at his skin and clothes as he rushed to find the other two. He stumbled and fell onto the ground and as he pulled himself up he suddenly saw Happy and Scorp sitting facing away from the advancing squadron, seemingly oblivious to any threat.

"Come on, quick!" shouted Logan, pulling at Scorp's sleeve. "Hoverhornets!" and he pointed to the horizon, where they could be seen approaching slowly, droning backwards and forwards in a pincer move.

"They're searching for us!" he shouted. "Quick! We've found a cave over there."

"Too late," shouted Scorp. "It's better to stay here amongst the cactus. At least we're partly hidden."

"No," shouted Logan. "It's better to be underground. Come on, back to the cave."

The other two reluctantly followed him and as they ran Logan suddenly saw a metal object glint on the ground. He picked it up and realised it was a communication device, with its light flashing on the red button. He stared at it. "Where's this come from?" he said.

"We haven't got time now. Hurry," shouted Scorp.

Logan gazed in horror at the device, recalling RS752 telling him to leave the red button pressed on in order to send a signal to reveal his position on the Sandia

Mountains. "It's sending a signal," he shouted and pressed off the button, which stopped glowing red. He took out the laser gun from his pocket and pointed it at Scorp and Happy. "Get to the cave now!" he shouted.

They ran down the knoll and up the scree into the cave, Logan following with the weapon aimed at their backs.

"What's happening?" cried Consuelo. "What are you doing?"

"One of them is a traitor," Logan said. "Someone was sending a signal on this to the robots to show where we are," and he produced the communication device, making everyone gasp in horror.

"No, that can't be so," said Consuelo, her face shocked.

"I don't know where it came from," said Scorp. "I've never had a communication device."

Logan stared belligerently at Scorp and Happy. Outside the cave, approaching hoverhornets could be heard droning nearer and nearer. Poppy started sobbing and the five-year –old Violeta held her hand. "Don't cry," she said "I won't let them hurt you."

Logan held Honey close to him, her dark chestnut hair against his hair, which was the same colour.

The hoverhornets were now almost above them. The noise was deafening and everyone clasped their hands to their ears. Consuelo was trembling and Sky put his arms around her. The noise increased and then slowly moved away. The group waited in silence as the droning faded, until it sounded more like a distant swarm of bees than a fleet of military aircraft.

"They've gone," said Logan and he looked round at everyone, amazement and relief showing on all their faces, as well as his own.

"It's surprising that they've gone," said Consuelo, voicing everyone's thoughts. "They obviously did not see the hoverbus."

"I turned off the communication device. Perhaps they couldn't then locate us," Logan said, glaring at Happy and Scorp.

"Which of you did it?" he shouted, glaring at them.

Happy giggled, as he often did, his cherub face with his bright, blue eyes, bursting into a smile.

"It's not Happy," said Consuelo. "It's obviously not him."

The group turned to look at Scorp, who stared defensively back at them.

"It wasn't me," he said calmly. "It must be Happy."

"You're lying," accused Logan.

"No, I'm not," said Scorp, his manner slightly less confident than usual.

"You want to be in a cage for the rest of your life, do you?" said Logan. "You want to be just an exhibit for the robots to look at, like a dodo or a woolly mammoth?"

"It wasn't me! I told you. I don't know where it came from. Perhaps someone else dropped it before us!"

"Don't be stupid," said Logan. "We're in the middle of nowhere. Who do you think has been wandering round here with a communication device which has been turned on to give a signal?"

Logan's temper flared and he punched Scorp in the face. Scorp retaliated and the two of them wrestled frantically on the floor of the cave, before rolling outside and falling down the scree, their bodies mixed up together, but still managing to hit each other. They landed at the bottom and Logan stood up wearily, flailing his arms at Scorp. Scorp retreated and Consuelo came running down the slope after them.

"Stop! Stop!" she said breathlessly, "I'm sure it's a mistake. We need to stay together and not fight."

Sky followed close behind her and he grabbed Logan as he was about to aim another punch, and Moon held Scorp. Scorp's lip was cut and bleeding whilst Logan's face was bruised and swollen. He sat down on the ground and Consuelo put her arms around him.

"I think we should wait in the cave until nightfall," she said. "It's too dangerous out in the open, now that the robots appear to be tracking us."

They did what Consuelo suggested and stayed quietly in the cave. The younger children quickly became bored and Consuelo sat telling them a story about a rabbit which was going to the moon in a big spaceship.

Happy was mischievous and jolly as normal, but Scorp sat at the side of the cave by himself, every so often looking curiously at Happy.

He came up to Logan and said to him, "I'm sorry about the fight. Can I have a word with you in private?"

Logan saw Happy glance curiously at them. He kept his hand on the laser gun in his pocket and motioned to Scorp to step outside the cave. They stood together, Logan keeping his distance, his mistrust showing on his battered and bruised face, and looking suspiciously at Scorp, whose face was equally battered and bruised.

"You don't believe me," said Scorp. "But I know it wasn't me. And therefore I know it has to be Happy!"

Logan stared. "Don't try and manipulate me," he said. "I don't trust you and nor does anyone else," and he motioned for him to go back into the cave. Scorp silently returned to his former seat and spent his time staring at Happy. Everyone else was subdued and the only excitement came when Violeta started poking a stick into a hole and Logan rushed forward to pull her away.

"There's a web covering the hole and that generally means there's a Black Widow spider in there," he said. "Don't go near it."

A red sun sank low on the horizon, but the evening was still warm. Logan and Consuelo handed round the food and drink they had brought and everyone sat quietly eating, after which Poppy and Moon fell asleep. The blackness of night descended, with its attendant cries. A coyote howled, and scampering and scurrying sounded from the gully.

"It's time to go," said Logan, and they all scrambled down the slippery slope and clambered into the hoverbus.

A huge moon hung luminously in a clear sky sparkling with star constellations.

"We're going up there," said Violeta, looking up. "We'll be there tomorrow."

Chapter 20

It was eerie buzzing along in the darkness. The headlights caught strange creatures flying and fluttering in its beam, and the scrubland below was also frequented by weird animals whose eyes glittered as they stared up at them and whose coats or skins had a ghostly hue.

Everyone else fell asleep except for Consuelo who sat next to Logan, talking softly to him to ensure that he stayed awake. They kept glancing anxiously around them, but hoverhornets did not appear, nor any other vehicle, for the whole route.

They arrived at the rendez-vous and Logan slowly lowered the hoverbus onto the ground. He and Consuelo climbed swiftly out of the vehicle and sat on the ground, shivering in the cold night.

Logan looked up at the moon and stars in the clear sky and said, "There's something wrong. I can feel it. I'm sure there's something wrong."

"What do you mean?" asked Consuelo.

"It's too easy," replied Logan. "Nothing has stopped us. The hoverhornets flew near, but not overhead. If they had, they would have seen the hoverbus. We were not stopped at the school or at the Human Baby Factory. It's strange."

"Well, nearly all the robots have been taken to California to help with the earthquake," said Consuelo.

"Yes, I suppose so," said Logan, shrugging his shoulders.

He thought for a moment, then said, "There's something else. When I spoke to RS752 in San Francisco it was almost as though he was saying goodbye to me, that he knew I was going."

Consuelo looked at him. "We will soon know if the Space Shuttle arrives. But if it all goes wrong and we're captured and taken back to Albuquerque, I hope we can be together."

Logan reached out and held her hand. "Yes, that's what I want as well."

A scorpion scuttled over the sand in front of them and they hastily stood up and retreated towards the hoverbus, where everyone was stretching and waking up. They all jumped out of the vehicle and sat together, watching as the sun rose, creating a pale yellow sky tinged with pink, and gazed in awe at the shining white expanse of sand revealed around them, the gypsum dunes shimmering as far as the horizon.

Violeta played with Honey, chasing her. Everyone else was more sombre, fear on their faces.

Scorp spoke for the others when he said, "It's all a hoax. We've been brought here for nothing. We'll just be captured and put back in the zoo again. No one is going to rescue us and take us to the moon. It's just a fantasy that Logan has dreamed up."

"The Shuttle is arriving at ten o' clock," repeated Logan, his face showing his own worry and uncertainty.

"There it is," he suddenly shouted, pointing upwards to a pale body streaking towards the earth. It roared downwards and landed bumpily, its long body racing across the flat sands. It almost skidded, but then corrected its trajectory and came to a gradual halt. The humans stared open-mouthed, their eyes wide, as the door opened and steps clattered down. A tall, dark-haired man in a grey uniform appeared, ran down the steps and strode up to them.

"Welcome," he said. "I'm Colonel Tolstoy and you're Logan, I believe," he said, addressing Logan. "We talked yesterday. Would you all please get quickly on board."

"Yes, we will," said Logan, smiling in relief.

He looked towards the horizon, where there was still no sign of any hoverhornets, and stood at the bottom of the steps, whilst Consuelo went first into the Space Shuttle, carrying Honey and holding Violeta's hand. The rest of the girls followed, then Sky and Moon. Colonel Tolstoy turned to Logan and remarked, "I thought you said there were earthquakes and tsunamis in California?"

"Yes, nearly all the robots have left Albuquerque to help the disaster area," he replied.

"You're completely misinformed," replied Colonel Tolstoy. "We have been monitoring the area from the moon, after you told us that, and there have definitely been no earthquakes or tsunamis in California."

Logan stared at him. "You must be wrong," he said. "All the robots have gone to help. There's no doubt."

"No, you're mistaken," Colonel Tolstoy replied. "But it's not important, surely?"

Logan stood on the steps and glanced at Happy who was picking up his bag. Colonel Tolstoy looked down from the entrance to the shuttle and said, "I'm sorry. Nothing extra. We already have a problem with the weight load."

Happy looked sullenly at him, then took a small glass tube from the bag and slipped it into his pocket.

Logan stared, his mind racing. He thought of computer-generated images of an earthquake. He remembered the bridge over the Rio Grande named after the scientist who had invented a new covering for robots, called skin, and that Happy never seemed to eat anything. He remembered the door of RS752's study left open so that he was able to enter it and see the video screens. He remembered RS752 dropping him near to the Human History Archives building the day of the storm and he thought again how easy it had been to rescue Scorp and Moon from the zoo, steal a hoverbus and bring everyone to White Sands. He thought of the robot he had lasered, which had perhaps malfunctioned by challenging them. He thought of the communication device sending the signal, and suddenly realised it was to show the hoverhornets their position, so that the robots could give the impression of searching, but not actually fly over them. And lastly, he thought of the Trojan Horse entering Troy and killing everyone.

He looked at Happy. "You're Trojan!" he said. "We were the ones who named you Happy. The robots want us to escape. It's always been their plan. They haven't created us to watch the behaviour of humans growing up. They've created us to kill the remaining humans on Mars and the Moon. They've pushed us into escaping and helped us to do it. They've even removed the force field so that the Space Shuttle can land and take off."

Consuelo appeared at the top of the steps. "What's the matter?" she asked. "Why aren't you coming?"

Logan took out the laser gun and aimed it at Happy.

"No," screamed Consuelo. "What are you doing?"

"You're wrong," said Happy, his cherub face with its blue eyes smiling mischievously at Logan whilst, at the same time, his hand was removing the flask from his pocket and opening its lid.

"Stop," shouted Logan. "You've got the deadly virus there which killed all the humans on Earth!"

He fired at Happy who fell backwards, his skin tearing, revealing his robot circuitry which fell out onto the ground. His arm, however, was still working, twitching as he held it up and threw the flask towards the open door of the Shuttle. Scorp immediately flung himself down from the steps, landing on top of both Happy and the flask.

"Go," he shouted, "before the virus escapes. I'm contaminated now. You've got to leave me."

Consuelo rushed inside and Logan and Colonel Tolstoy bounded up the steps, the door immediately locking behind them. The Space Shuttle raced across the gypsum sands and accelerated up into the sky. Logan looked through the window and saw Scorp far below, saluting the vehicle. He shakily saluted back, then strapped himself into his seat, as the Space Shuttle shot upwards, leaving behind the gleaming brilliance of the white sands. The Shuttle roared through the atmosphere and Logan glanced contentedly at Consuelo sitting on one side of him and Honey on the other, and then looked down at Earth, where clouds were delicately trailing across its blueness.

"We have freedom now," he said, "and one day we will return to reclaim our world."

Printed in Great Britain
by Amazon

33830931R00076